FAMILY VOICES
A MONTREAL STORY

FAMILY VOICES

A MONTREAL STORY

Rita J. Beron

Copyright © 2003 by Rita J. Beron.

Library of Congress Number:		2003095680
ISBN:	Hardcover	1-4134-2576-3
	Softcover	1-4134-2575-5

All rights reserved. No part of this book may be reproduced or transmitted in any form or by any means, electronic or mechanical, including photocopying, recording, or by any information storage and retrieval system, without permission in writing from the copyright owner.

This book was printed in the United States of America.

To order additional copies of this book, contact:
Xlibris Corporation
1-888-795-4274
www.Xlibris.com
Orders@Xlibris.com
20781

CONTENTS

PROLOGUE: SETTING THE SCENE 7
CHAPTER I : MONTREAL 1885 17
CHAPTER II : MONTREAL 1915 33
CHAPTER III : GILBERTE'S VOICE 55
CHAPTER IV : LAURETTE'S VOICE 65
CHAPTER V : GERARD'S VOICE 69
CHAPTER VI : EMILIENNE'S VOICE 77
CHAPTER VII : GERMAINE'S VOICE 83
CHAPTER VIII : SIMONE'S VOICE 89
CHAPTER IX : CECILE'S VOICE 97
CHAPTER X : DIANA'S VOICE 101
THE FINAL CHAPTER 114
EPILOGUE 123
ACKNOWLEDGMENTS
    AND RESEARCH READING 127
FURTHER ACKNOWLEDGMENTS 129
SYNOPSIS OF FAMILY VOICES 131

PROLOGUE

Setting the Scene

I decided before I started writing the story of my grandmother and her family, I would first do research into the conditions she and her family experienced in their every day lives in the early 1900s. Since my knowledge of the earliest French Canadian history was also limited, I realized I wanted to know more. So my research took on a new dimension that led me to Montreal and many archival libraries. I will only be able to give you a brief sketch of the earliest history. It will lack many of the details, because from what I have learned, it would make up an entire book. But I would like you to understand something of what preceded her life, and what my own ancestors went through to exist. I will start with the earliest of the white men who touched on the North American continent from which there is some documentation, either written or verbally presented.

John Cabot was born in Venice, but spent much of his life in England, when he set out with a commission from King Henry V11 on May 2nd 1497, only five years after Columbus's discovery. He was the first white man to see the mainland of the North American continent. Since no records were kept, except what he verbally expressed when he returned, it is believed that he sailed along the coast of Labrador, and possibly Newfoundland.

But it wasn't until 1534, that Jacque Cartier, with a commission from King Francis I of France, directed an exploring expedition that led the way up the St. Lawrence. He uncovered vast areas of land and many lakes that before were unknown to the white man.

Then in 1603, Champlain began his exploration of North America. He entered into an accord with the tribes known as the Algonquins to promote peace, and as a result of his efforts, he founded Quebec in 1608. Of the original 28 settlers, only eight survived the first year. They were poorly equipped and not prepared for the cold. The starvation was inevitable when their meager supplies ran out, and the diseases came with the weakening of their bodies. Had it not been for the Indians, none of the first settlers would have survived. Ships arrived in June of 1609 with men and supplies, and it gave renewed hope to the survivors.

Samuel de Champlain was the most important figure in the internal exploration of Canada and it was he who pioneered the colonies. Cartier started the exploration of the St. Lawrence, but Champlain accomplished the practical work and the systematic examination of the interior. He lived a rugged life, one of explorer and colonizer until his early death in 1635. He had great natural skills as a geographer. His ability to piece together all of his knowledge, to understand and clarify the relationship of the St. Lawrence and all of the Great Lakes waterways, is shown in his maps of 1632, and it was a major accomplishment recognized by the world.

As the years went by, the long standing hostility between France and Britain in Europe that had existed for hundreds of years, was heightened in North America by a growing rivalry over the Newfoundland fisheries and the fur trade of the continental interior. The active and curious French took an early lead and throughout the seventeenth century, they explored all of the areas to the Great Plains and the mouth of the Mississippi.

It was in the early 1640s that my own ancestors emigrated from Normandy, and the western part of France, to settle in the new colony in what is now Quebec. My ancestor on my grandfather's side was a navigator, named Antoine Pepin, who decided to stay because he liked the possibilities of the freedoms that he felt New France represented.

In 1666, the Marquis de Tracy eliminated the danger of the Iroquois and there was rapid progress after that date. Talon, Colbert and Frontenac were responsible for pushing the growth and development of the villages. In the 18th century La Verendryes and others led the way out into the Great Plains.

The English were slow in pushing inland from Hudson Bay and what they did accomplish was often with the assistance of Frenchmen like Radisson and Jean Couture and Dutchmen like Viele. The English were happy to let the endlessly curious and vigorous French do the exploring which was costly and could be life threatening. As a result of this, they made very few recorded journeys, but there were many important men who played a crucial role in the discovery of the continent. These men remain almost totally unrecognized by history, such as Radisson, Groseilliers, Dulhut, Tonti and many other missionaries, coureurs de bois, and Indian guides whose bravery and resourcefulness helped them accomplish these goals.

Of the French kings, Francis 1st and Henry 4th were both considered kings who were open and receptive patrons of exploration and colonization, particularly of Canada. Of the English and Canada, Henry V11 encouraged the Cabots and James 1st was a patron of Lord Selkirk. Henry V111 and Elizabeth promoted maritime discovery, but Canada did not benefit from their efforts.

Throughout the years of struggle in New France, a strong people developed. There were many heroes, and many great deeds were accomplished. There were also some scoundrels who came to govern, sometimes from the courts of the king of France, who openly took advantage of the people for their own gain. They came and went, but the families survived and their survival became part of the ongoing sagas that have been carried down by generations and are recounted today as family legends. They survived the hardships that came from the land. They counted their blessings and rejoiced in the freedoms they experienced: the freedom to fish, to hunt, to work the soil and produce what they needed.

They were a gay people, full of piety and pride and they loved their music and dance. Their children were healthier than they had been in France. The English noted that so many of the French settlers seemed to be adept at learning other languages. It was common for families to speak many dialects of Indian and as new settlers came into the area, they seemed to understand them as well. Their own language was Norman French. Perhaps, because they mixed freely with the native Indians, and other emigrants that they met. They recognized very early on that they had much to learn from each other. The natives had shown the first settlers how to wrap their feet during winter when they had inadequate clothing and shoes and this became a tradition that carried down to the time of Pehr Kalm's visit in 1749, for he noted it in his diaries. The strong stone houses they built, the music they loved, and the piety and fairness they exhibited toward their neighbors seemed to characterize their culture, and they became the organizing rules of law and society in New France. In the early 1700s the population of New France tripled to 45,000. Most of them were now born in Canada, and a great percentage of the growing population lived along the banks of the St. Lawrence. Pehr Kalm, a Swedish botanist who visited the area in 1749 commented, "The colony was really one continued village, with fine houses of stone, large grain fields, meadows, pastures, woods of deciduous trees and some churches." This was strung out for 200 miles along both sides of the river, linked mainly by families and networks of families. Pehr Kalm continued in his diary, "One can scarcely find in a city in other parts, people who treat one with such politeness both in word and deed as is true everywhere in the homes of the peasants in Canada. I traveled in various places during my stay in this country. I frequently happened to take up my abode for several days at the homes of peasants where I had never been before, and who had never heard of nor seen me and to whom I had no letters of introduction. Nevertheless they showed me wherever I came a devotion paid ordinarily to a native or relative."

In comparing them to their counterparts in France, a French officer noted that "They would be scandalized to be called peasants. In fact, they are of better stuff, have more wit, more education than those of France. This comes from paying no taxes, that they have the right to hunt and fish, and that they live in a sort of independence."

RITA J. BERON

During the last of the 1600s and the early 1700s there was much fighting between the English, the French Canadians and the Indians, the Indians changing sides when it seemed to them to be advantageous. The English badly wanted a foothold on the North American continent. They wanted Canada because it would strike a death blow at the empire of France. Canada was an excellent field for settlement and it would be a valuable market for British produce.

King Louis XV sent more than six thousand soldiers from France between 1755 and 1759 to save his American Empire. The borders between New France or what we now know as Quebec and the British colonies in the New England states were obscure, often changing daily. The fighting in America in the New England colony between the rebels and the British, and the British and the French in New France had been going on a couple of years before France and England again declared war. It was a confusing time. The soldiers that France sent to help the rebels in the New England were effectual, and eventually helped the New England colony to gain independence from England. The soldiers from France who came to help save New France for the French Empire were frustrated, because the French in New France were taught to fight by the Indians, and their ways were different. Instead of kneeling and firing on command, they would scatter, as the Indians had taught them. They were successful on their own, as they were in 1755 when fewer than a thousand French from New France and Indian allies held the Ohio against more than three times as many British and colonial soldiers. But later in New France, the British stepped up their efforts. As a result, in 1759, Wolfe captured Quebec bringing the struggle to an end. In 1763, Canada and adjacent possessions were transferred to British rule.

The difference of cultures and religion placed Canada in a difficult position. The prior treaty rights the French Canadians had entered into demanded recognition. So two principles entered into the form of government: (1) the establishment of a new British settlement, (2) and the preservations of the rights of the French Canadians.

On Oct. 7, 1763, General Murray was entrusted with the civil government of the Province of Quebec. Murray was assisted by a council composed of the leading officers of government, many of them were the officers left from the war, together with 8 persons chosen by the governor from the inhabitants of the province. The old army officers who had worked with Murray during the period of its military rule, had a great sympathy for the early French inhabitants. These military men had been proud of their own profession, but they had contempt for the vulgar commercial classes, who were arriving with great frequency from Great Britain, and with good reason. Of the British who were coming in to make their fortunes as traders, some were honest, but most were chiefly adventurers who had failed or accomplished little in their own country and they cared little about the means, provided the ends they desired were obtained. Murray called them the most immoral collection of men he had ever known.

In a quote from Sir Guy Carleton to Hillsborough on March 28, 1770, he said, "The abuses perpetrated on an ignorant and submissive people under the pretext of administration of justice were a disgrace to British citizenship. In French Canada after the Conquest, as elsewhere and at other times, the greatest hindrance to the Anglicizing of the community were the Englishmen. In our endeavors to establish the loyalty of French Canada to the British crown on a firm and natural basis we were compelled to be constantly on our guard against the rapacity of our fellow countrymen." Illegal seizures of property and exorbitant fees in the settlement of minor debts were common practice with many homes and lands being seized. Carleton eventually succeeded in designing a law that defeated the plans of these immoral individuals.

In 1774, the French Canadian was granted the rights to a free and unmolested existence by the British government. In 1791, it gave French Canada a system of government that was incompatible with the principles of nationalism. A conflict was inevitable.

Upper Canada was a British Community shorn of its ancestral aristocratic tendencies. In 1791, Upper Canada was granted a constitution modeled on the aristocracy and on the British

Constitution. The external form of the British Constitution was granted, but its substance was withheld. The real genius and spirit of British parliamentary institutions were denied to the overseas subjects of the empire. The government fell into the hands of many bigoted and avaricious men. It was impossible that an intelligent and vigorous people, both English and French, would submit to incompetent leadership. Here also a struggle was unavoidable. The colonies demanded self-government. The political revolution of 1837 was only the beginning of the growing pains necessary before Canada would attain its freedom. It was necessary for the British to change their vision of a colonial empire. They had to rearrange the tools that were the basis of governance, because the empire had been sustained on an artificial basis. Colonial independence became the sacrifice that was needed to preserve the unity of the Empire and became the foundation of imperial unity in other colonies as well.

By the early 1800s, Montreal was becoming a major power and commercial center. Its position of dominance in economic life in the Dominion was directly related to two facts. Montreal was located on the St. Lawrence River which made it possible to become a great shipping center and inland port, and the overabundance of inexpensive labor made it easier to become a great manufacturing center.

In 1817 Britain sent in the Scots to organize the bank of Montreal. They formed a system of chartered banks with branches throughout the major cities of Canada that gave the entire banking system a badly needed stability and mutual support. The bank printed its own notes that provided the needed capital for all of the commercial transactions that a young growing country goes through. By 1900, assets and volume of business were as important as any bank in New York. Montreal remained a major power and commercial center for almost a hundred years.

In the 1890s, there were 50 to 150 people in Montreal, many of them Scots, who owned two thirds of the wealth of the entire nation of Canada. It was interesting because they never considered themselves Canadian as much as they felt they were British. They were mainly segregated (they segregated themselves) in an area of

Montreal called the Square Mile. They emulated the grandeur of the lives of the British aristocracy. They built elaborate mansions and staffed them with a full retinue of servants, including cooks, maids and butlers, errand boys, and gardeners. They also employed a nurse, nanny and a governess for their children. Had they stayed in Great Britain, these opportunities would not have been available to them. Their children were sheltered and unaware of another life and existence not far from where they lived.

Many of these men were geniuses of a kind, and they invested in many kinds of businesses. They paid the people (mostly French Canadians and other immigrants as well) who worked in the factories as little as they could. They considered it "only good business sense." There were also smaller business owners, some French and some Jews, who took advantage of these prevalent business practices. More often than not, what they paid them was less than half of the poverty rate that existed in the United States at the same time. Child labor was rampant. Twelve-hour days, six days a week were typical in the early 1900s. In the banking systems that had developed in Montreal, it was only through years of nepotism, and the arrogance of believing that their judgments were always superior to the judgments of others, that the power eventually passed to Toronto in the mid-twentieth century. Some would insist that it was also the westward development of Canada that made the power pass to Toronto. In fact, both of these explanations are true. Young entrepreneurs were forced to go to Toronto to borrow money for future business projects, whether it was a railroad to ship lumber or a proposed mine.

Now, imagine yourself in the late 1800s in Montreal and I will tell you of my grandmother.

Diana Roberts — Age 4

CHAPTER I

MONTREAL 1885

"To cease to be loved is for the child practically synonymous with ceasing to live."
      Dr. Karl Menninger—A Psychiatrist's World

The large gray stone mansion on the hill seemed more like a castle to Diana but she shuddered when she looked at it through the small carriage window, as the horses pulled the carriage through the winding roadway ahead. It was autumn and the trees in the gardens around the house had lost their leaves and the bare branches were bending with the force of the wind. To her it seemed frightening and cold.

Suddenly the horses and the carriage stopped on the circular drive near the front entrance. The door opened and a round faced man in a black suit with a dimpled smile and a twinkle in his eyes, emerged and walked down the steps to meet her. A prim young lady in a gray dress with a high white collar was at this side. Four year old Diana could not quite reach the bottom step of the carriage, so the gentleman helped her down, all the while introducing himself. "I am Hilliard, the butler, Miss Diana, and this young woman is your governess, Mademoiselle Morin. Welcome to 'Chez Des Jardins.'"

"I am happy to meet you Hilliard." She smiled at the governess, "And I am happy to meet you Mademoiselle Morin."

"Come with me, Miss Diana, and I will show you to your rooms." Mlle. Morin took Diana's hand and they walked up the stairs and through the tall double doors into the grand foyer. The ceiling seemed exceptionally high to Diana and the windows were scenes of flowers and trees, beautifully depicted in varying shades of greens and yellows in stained glass. Diana was still busy looking at the lovely windows when her governess led her into the large room ahead. Diana could see a wide curving staircase at the end of the vast room. Though the room was sparsely furnished with tables and lamps and groups of chairs placed in comfortable settings, it seemed to Diana that it must be the palace of a princess. She felt that she should be on tip-toes and quiet because she was intruding in this huge room, and she knew she did not belong there. They walked past a tall fireplace, the scale of which matched the twenty-foot ceilings. Diana was dwarfed by the height of the andirons, and she noticed that the opening in the fireplace was much higher than a tall man's head.

As they climbed up the marble stairway with the curving brass balustrade at the end of the grand room, Diana couldn't help noticing the many paintings of men and women, all strangers to her, on the walls. "Who are all of these people, Mlle. Morin?"

"I have been told that all of the people you see here are your ancestors."

"Ancestors? I didn't know I had any." Diana looked up as Mlle. Morin smiled.

"Everyone has ancestors. I have quite a few myself, though perhaps they are not as illustrious as these."

"What does illustrious mean?" Diana looked puzzled.

Mlle. Morin smiled, "Why, it means that your ancestors were very distinguished. They were people of character and achievement." They walked up a smaller wooden stairway to the third floor and stopped before a white door.

"Here is your bedroom and your bath, Diana, and as soon as you have had a chance to look it over and wash up a bit, I will take you down stairs to see Monsieur and Madame Desjardin." She paused, "Diana, they are so happy you are here. I know that this is all so new to you, but I don't want you to be nervous or afraid. I have the bedroom next to yours," Mlle. Morin walked to her own door and opened it and showed Diana how close she would be, "and I can leave my door open at night if you wish. I want you to feel at home here and to know you can come to me at any time if you have questions, or if you are lonely or afraid."

"Thank you, Mlle. Morin. You are kind. May I ask you a question?"

"Of course, anytime."

Diana went on in a small voice, "When I say your name, Mademoiselle Morin, it makes me feel I will always be a stranger. I would like to know if I may call you by your first name? Would you think it disrespectful of me?"

"No, I would not. You may call me Mademoiselle Amy."

"Thank you, I like the name Amy. Mademoiselle Amy . . . yes, I like the way it sounds." Diana looked back, saying she would wash her face and brush her hair and would be ready in a few minutes to meet the Desjardins.

On the way down stairs to the library where the Desjardins were waiting, Diana was feeling nervous and sick. "What if they don't like me, Mlle. Amy? They may not like me at all. But maybe . . . maybe if that happens . . . I could go home again." Diana's look indicated she was very close to tears.

"From what I understand, Monsieur Desjardin loves you very much. And both he and Madame are very happy you are here. Don't be afraid, Diana. You will see that I am right."

The Desjardins were sitting in large chintz upholstered chairs near the fireplace in the library. "Come here, child, come and let me look at you." Albina Desjardin smiled as she held out her hand to Diana.

Diana placed her small hand in Madame Desjardins' hand. "I am very pleased to meet you. And I hope you like me."

"Of course I like you. We hope you will be very happy here, Diana."

"My mother asked me to be brave. I know I will miss my family, but I will try." She managed to get through the short visit, by smiling a lot and saying little, and trying not to think of the home she had left.

As Diana made herself ready for bed that evening, she cried when she thought of her mother. She could not understand why she was being sent to live with an uncle whom she had not seen often in her life. She knew he was her paternal grandmother's brother, because that had been explained to her over and over again, and that he had always wanted a daughter of his own. She was told she would be educated like a queen, and she had always been his favorite. But she missed her maman and papa and her three little sisters. She remembered what her mother had told her, when she had left. Her maman had tears in her eyes when she had said that she would always love her, but that one day she would realize it was for the best. That Uncle Georges could give her so much more than they could. Diana wanted to shout, "But I want to be home with you, Maman. Please don't send me away."

Eventually the tears stopped and she slipped into a troubled sleep.

The next morning, she was awakened by the sound of singing birds. Sunlight flooded her room and it was the first time she took notice of her bedroom. Every thing seemed to be bathed in a golden glow. She had a large four poster bed that was very high off the floor. It had a feather mattress, and down pillows and soft silky quilts in pale yellow. The walls were papered in a yellow print with small white roses. Her bedroom dresser was in dark wood with lace doilies and there was a small bouquet of white and yellow roses on one end. She ran to the windows to see if she could see the birds that were singing so sweetly. She couldn't see the birds, but she could feel the soft breeze coming into her room. Apartment living in the city had not prepared her for the feelings she had now when she looked out at nature in every direction. Her bedroom was in the west wing of the third floor. Connected to her room was Mlle. Amy's room. Down the hall a large third room was used for classroom studies and music lessons. Diana ran from room to room, looking out of the large windows in all of the rooms. All had a view of the gardens below, and manicured lawns and trees. From her bedroom, she could see all of the landscaped flower beds, the remnants of remaining fall flowers still filling the gardens with vibrant color. The bare branches of the trees in the distance presented an elegant lace work against the bright blue of the sky. The view from the study room was different. She could see a pond with a small waterfall at one end. And when the windows were open she could hear the silvery sounds as the water rippled over the rocks into the pool. There was also a table and chairs on a bricked patio under a tree with low hanging branches, the leaves on the ground gently blowing with the wind. The stone stables where the horses and carriages were kept were also visible from where she stood. She wished her sisters were with her to see it. But no matter how lovely this home was, she yearned to be back home in a small bedroom that she had shared with her three younger sisters. She wanted her maman and her papa. The tears came and spilled down her cheeks, just as Mlle. Amy knocked on her door.

"I see you are up bright and early. The gardens are lovely, aren't they?" Mlle. Amy then noticed the tears. "Oh Diana, come here to me." She took Diana in her arms.

Diana wiped her tears with her hand, "I was just thinking of my sisters. I miss them. I probably will always miss them. It is not that I don't appreciate what they want to do for me here, but I don't really understand it. How could my own maman and my papa give me away?"

"My dear Diana, I don't know all of the reasons, but perhaps one day you will understand."

A few months after, the teary episodes were fewer, but Diana had grown thinner, and Mlle. Morin was concerned enough to be constantly vigilant for signs of things she especially enjoyed. Diana loved to eat in the kitchen with the servants. It was always cozy and informal there and everyone was kind to her. They treated her in a warm, unceremonious way that made her feel at home. She liked the cook who always had a hug for her, and always encouraged her to eat. The cook's name was Flannery. Her rosy dimpled face was always smiling. She was also quite rotund, and Diana felt a special comfort when Flannery would pick her up

FAMILY VOICES

and cuddle her. Flannery always called her, "My sweet lamb." Though the Desjardins frowned upon having Diana eat in the kitchen, they had not said or done anything overt that forbade her from doing so, and Mlle. Morin took every advantage she could to see that Diana ate well and laughed like a child should.

One day when Mlle. Morin and Diana were eating in the kitchen, a man Diana had not met before delivered groceries and supplies. The servants seemed to know him very well. He was a large, heavy-set man with a ruddy complexion, and small eyes that were set too close together. His large mouth had thick lips, and some missing teeth. The servants called him Raoul.

"Raoul, would ye like some lovely stew for lunch? I have plenty, and ye can have as much as ye'd like." With that invitation from Flannery, Raoul sat down with all of his outer clothing on, even his hat, and picked up his knife and fork and dug in to the food that was piled high on the plate.

Diana watched with a great fascination. A fascination which soon turned to fear as she watched Raoul eat. He stuffed his mouth as one would who was starving, and afraid the food would be taken away. Some of the food spilled out of his mouth because he filled it beyond capacity. As he chewed, he repeatedly choked, sometimes requiring Flannery to pound him on the back, to loosen the food that was lodged in his throat. The food was ejected across the table with a well-placed hit on his back, and to Diana's complete dismay, this happened again and again. With every huge mouthful, the worry and the panic now etched in the lines on her small forehead became greater. Suddenly she was shouting, "Stop! Stop! Monsieur Raoul, there is a lot of food, please . . . please try to eat slower. Then you won't choke. I'm afraid . . ."

Albina Desjardins came into the kitchen in time to hear what Diana had said. "Diana, I cannot believe you would speak like that to your elders! You will go this moment and kneel on the servants' staircase with the door closed till I say you may come out. Perhaps that will teach you to think before you speak!"

Diana looked stricken; her lower lip trembled. The stairway

was dark if the door at the bottom of the stairway was closed. "Yes, mam. I didn't mean . . ."

"No excuses will be accepted, Diana. You must learn your place."

Mlle. Morin spoke up, "Madame Desjardins, I believe you misunderstood Diana's intention. She was deeply concerned that Monsieur Raoul would choke."

"You needn't trouble yourself, Mlle. Morin. Every child needs strict discipline. She must learn. And may I remind you, I am in charge." The look on Madame's face reflected the seriousness of her displeasure. "You may go to your quarters. I will see that Diana does not miss her classes this afternoon."

Mademoiselle Amy Morin looked at the classroom clock and wondered if she should go down and check on Diana. It had been far too long. Surely, Diana cannot still be kneeling on the dark stairway. But thoughts of a forgotten Diana made her go to check. It had now been four hours and she must find her. What if Madame had forgotten about her?

Madame Desjardins was reading in the library. She looked up when Mlle. Morin entered.

"I was concerned when Diana did not come for any of her classes. I felt compelled to check, Madame Desjardins. It is not like her to miss her classes. She has a true love of learning. I waited this long to check because I thought that, perhaps, you wanted to spend some time with her."

As the truth of the situation seemed to sink in, the look on Madame Desjardins face changed to one of shock. Her hand flew to her mouth, "Oh no," she exclaimed, and promptly went to the kitchen to let Diana out. Mlle. Morin followed close behind. Madame opened the door to the servants' stairway. Diana was still kneeling, her face tear stained and swollen. She covered her eyes with her small hand and peeked out at the sun streaming through the kitchen curtains.

"Is it all right . . . may . . . may I come out now? Fresh tears were on her cheeks as she asked.

Madame Desjardins looked down at the small girl, "Yes, yes of course. I am sure you have learned your place."

FAMILY VOICES

Mademoiselle Morin took Diana by the hand and said in a cheerful voice, "I think we may still have time for a lesson or two." Diana looked up with gratitude in her large gray eyes.

After the episode in the kitchen, Diana became more reticent, more reluctant to spend time in the kitchen with the people who loved her. She spent more time with her books and her dolls. She shared many personal thoughts with her doll Charlotte and admonished her to never speak harsh words to anyone. She would often dress her doll Charlotte and take her out on the patio where they would have a pretend tea party. Charlotte and she shared the secrets of her heart and her new life.

Mlle. Morin noted Diana's withdrawal with sadness, but continued her encouragement in every way that she could. Slowly the kitchen incident was forgotten, and Diana's normal behavior returned. Mlle. Amy was continually surprised and pleased that her young student excelled in all of her studies. She also learned that Diana had special gifts that the average child lacked. Her natural ability to sense the true feelings of people with whom she came in contact, was a character trait that remained with her all of her life.

The next two and a half years passed quickly. One evening when Diana was going to begin getting ready for bed, she heard a knock at her door. Mlle. Amy peeked into the room. "May I come in?"

"Yes, please do," Diana responded.

"Before you undress and get ready for bed, Madame and Monsieur Desjardins would like you to come down for a visit. They are in the library. Is that agreeable with you?"

"Yes . . . yes of course. Tell them I will be down in a few minutes."

As Diana walked down the long staircases, she wondered what she could expect. The Desjardins did not request a meeting unless it was for something serious. She had feelings of nausea as she entered the library.

Georges Desjardins looked up from the magazine he was reading. His wavy gray hair was neatly combed and his dark mustache was curled on the ends and made him look like he had a perpetual smile on his face. He spoke first, "Have you had a chance to consider what we discussed the last time we spoke? We would really appreciate it if you would call us Maman and Papa. We have discussed this often enough, and you must be aware we want to adopt you."

"If you adopted me, what would that mean to me? Would anything change?"

"It would mean that we would be your legal parents . . ."

Diana interrupted, "But I have parents . . ."

"We have never tried to take their place, only to better your life," Georges seemed perplexed. "So how do you feel?"

"I . . . I didn't have a choice when I came here. Everyone told me it was for my good. Even my maman told me the same thing. For a long time, I cried myself to sleep every night. I couldn't understand why my parents would give me away. And I kept hoping they would take me back. In fact, it has been only in the last month that I have realized it will never happen. And I finally understand why I was sent here. The last time my maman came for a visit, she told me my papa was very ill. I know he has never been healthy, but I know it will be hard for her if he dies.

"I am sorry, child, I did not know this. Your grandmother did not tell me." Albina wiped her eyes, and Georges took out his handkerchief and hastily wiped his nose.

"I feel I cannot call you maman and papa. But if I could call you Uncle Georges and Aunt Albina, it would seem so much closer and more like family for me. And it would seem natural for me to call you Aunt Albina because I have a younger sister who is named Albina. It is already a family name. May I do that? I hope you will not feel sad." Diana breathed a sigh of relief as she spoke that last sentence, as if it had been on her mind for a long time, but she could never make herself say it. Then she got up from the chair she was sitting in and put her arms around her Uncle Georges' neck, and did the same to her Aunt Albina. "Uncle Georges, and Aunt Albina . . . I think that sounds like a real family to me."

Uncle Georges took out his handkerchief again and openly dabbed at his eyes. He looked touched. Aunt Albina removed a handkerchief that was in her sleeve, and quickly wiped her eyes. She looked embarrassed to be seen with tears.

Diana suddenly realized that the hugs she had given her aunt and her uncle made her feel better. As she was leaving the library for bed, she ran back to kiss her aunt and uncle goodnight. "I hope you don't mind, because this is what families do, and I have been missing hugs and kisses from my family for a long time."

"Oh child, we are getting older and we are unaccustomed to having children around. Forgive us. I see that for all we have wanted to do for you, we have neglected you. Thank you for reminding us that we need hugs and kisses too. We will try to be more like a family."

Her Uncle Georges gave her an extra hug before he put her down.

"Mlle. Morin says that children are like special plants. We need food and water but to grow healthy, we need a loving family. Mlle. Morin has been a good teacher. She has helped me to understand and appreciate what you are doing for me, and she has been kind. She said I have become a mature seven year old."

"I am so happy that you have had Mlle. Morin to look after you. And I am realizing it takes more than providing for a child to be a parent." Albina put her hand on Diana's head as she spoke, while she looked into her eyes. "Thank you for coming to us. We did not realize how very much we have needed you, Diana."

"And I have needed you both to be my family." Diana looked back and waved as she left the room.

It was not long after this discussion that Diana's father died, and her grandmother was deeply concerned about the family, and how they would survive. Diana's father had never been a strong child, and her grandmother was partly responsible for the decision that her son and daughter-in-law made concerning the giving up of one of the children to her brother, Georges Desjardin, a wealthy business man, who had always wanted a daughter of his own. And several years after her son's death, it was she who introduced her daughter-in-law to a distant cousin named Joseph Desjardin, whom she later married. So that is how Diana's mother also came to be called Marie-Louise Pichette Robert Desjardin.

The Georges Desjardins, in keeping with their plan to give Diana an education fit for a princess, enrolled her in a boarding school the fall after her seventh birthday. She could come home on holidays and an occasional weekend but this was not allowed until the adjustment period was over for the individual student. The nuns did not favor the younger students going home to their parents every weekend because they felt it made their adjustment to the rigors and rules of convent life more difficult.

Mlle. Amy prepared Diana very well for the beginnings of school and Diana had been a reader since she was four. Her abilities in language were already far superior to other students her age and much older. The Sisters of Saint Croix were surprised when Diana's skills were tested to see what level of learning she had achieved.

The Convent of St. Laurent was far ahead of other convents in the city of Montreal, in their mission and their view of teaching principles. That is why it was a popular "finishing school" for young ladies of means. They were pushed to learn according to their abilities, and their achievements were notable. They were well versed in the arts and music, literature and philosophy, history, geography and mathematics, Latin and other languages, including French. They were also ahead in the teaching of hygiene and what they commonly called, "womanly skills," including art, needlework, cooking and flower arranging.

Diana's piano playing skills developed rapidly, and soon she was playing concerts in other churches in the city. When she was ten years old, she was considered the most talented piano student in the school, and soon requests for her talents came from agencies throughout the city. The Desjardins would not agree to have her play for the general public. They considered it appropriate for her to play only in a church setting.

She was intellectually blooming as well. The teachers at the Convent of St. Laurent, were constantly surprised when they discovered the level of her understanding of the philosophers, and her abilities to discuss the meaning of their work. Her work in literature and her other studies were equally outstanding.

Diana was happier than she had been. She had one or two close friends, and much to her joy, her aunt and uncle permitted her to visit her friend Rosa's home for an occasional weekend. Rosa's home was much closer to the school than her own. She felt freer there, and Rosa made her laugh. Rosa's family was a close-knit group. They were loud, demonstrative and considerate with each other. Diana secretly enjoyed being around all of the hugging and the children who always seemed to be talking at once. Rosa's brother Guy was three years older and he seemed awkward and shy around the girls, but he often took walks with them along the river, while he recited poetry. As Diana grew up, her friendship with Rosa remained strong. Guy's interest in poetry had become his life. And his poetry had appeared in numerous anthologies in Montreal and Quebec. He was studying literature and poetry with the hopes of becoming a teacher, but his serious interest continued to be his poetry. One Sunday afternoon when they were taking their usual walk by the river, he took Diana by the hand and asked his sister if he could speak to Diana alone.

Rosa did not look surprised, but she answered, "Of course," she walked about twelve feet away from them and sat on a bench near a picnic table. She was trying to look disinterested as she strained to hear what they were saying to each other.

Guy faced Diana, and took both of her hands in his. "Dear Diana, I never thought I would be able to speak of this because it is so close to my heart, but I have thought of it for a long time." He hesitated for a moment, looked away as if gathering his thoughts, and continued. "I have loved you from the first day that I met you, and I realize you have not been aware of it, but I wanted to speak to you of my feelings for you. You and Rosa will graduate from school in a few months and I wanted to know what you are planning. Will you go on to a university next fall, or will you become a professional pianist?" Guy looked serious and his gaze was intense.

Diana seemed completely taken by surprise, but she spoke gently, "Thank you for saying that. I feel honored that you love me. I know you feel you know me, just from the conversations we have shared since we were very young. Perhaps you do, but I . . . I am not really sure what love is. I have always liked you Guy. You have a kindness in you and a sensitivity that is reflected in your poetry. But I honestly don't know what my future holds. You know that I have lived with my Aunt Albina and Uncle Georges, and we have not discussed any future plans. My Aunt Albina is quite ill now and I am not sure if that will have a bearing on my future or not. I will be eighteen next June after I graduate."

With only six weeks until graduation and her aunt's deteriorating health, the next weekends were spent in her home, with her aunt and her uncle. Diana did not realize that suddenly she would be faced with a challenging change.

The dining room was looking especially beautiful with the firelight and the soft candles glowing on the sparkling linens. The floor was marble, covered with brightly colored oriental rugs, and the ceiling was of wood, very high with dark beams. It was one of the last Sunday evenings at dinner, before Diana was to go back to school. Her Aunt Albina was too ill to come down to dinner, and her doctor was at her side. Uncle Georges sat across from her looking extremely uncomfortable. He would start to say something; then he would stammer, look down at his plate and stop. He folded and unfolded his napkin as if he needed to do something, anything to keep from having to say what he needed to say. "What is it Uncle Georges? I know you have been trying to say something to me all during our dinner. What is it that has made you so distraught?"

"Your aunt and I have been discussing the fact that she will not be here much longer, and she feels that it would not be acceptable for you to live in this house with me after she is gone. She feels that people will talk, since you are not our legally adopted daughter. Perhaps . . . perhaps not adopting you was a major mistake. We never considered that this could happen." Uncle Georges seemed despondent.

FAMILY VOICES

"I never thought of a situation like this either. But what exactly did you have in mind?" Diana's voice was on edge, like she did not know what to expect.

"Your aunt wants me to find you a good husband."

"A husband? You can't be serious." Diana flushed at the thought.

"But I am very serious, and it must be decided soon."

"To marry someone I don't even know is something I will never consider."

"Understand this my girl, you will not have a choice. Can't you see the logic of it? Your reputation would be ruined if you remain with me. And that could ruin your life."

"But that seems so . . . so old fashioned and barbaric to force me to marry someone I don't know. It's 1899! We are coming into a new age and a new century. Why can't I go out and find an apartment and some kind of suitable work? I am quite capable, more than you can imagine. I know I could do it."

"It is just not proper for you to do such a thing. You are too young to be on your own. I know of no young women of good families who go out and work."

"Uncle Georges, you just said I am too young to be on my own, but somehow you don't think I am too young to be married, and have responsibility to a husband and perhaps a family one day. That doesn't make sense to me."

"But don't you see, Diana, that it would be the proper way for a young woman of refinement. I will not have you marry just anyone."

"So I will have no say in the matter?" Diana looked up in disbelief as she realized her uncle was serious. She burst into tears, left the dining room and ran up the stairs to her room, leaving Uncle Georges bewildered.

"Don't you see, Diana, that this is the only proper answer," said Georges Desjardins to the empty chair across from him. He was frantic as he thought of her reaction. I could arrange some kind of party where they could meet under more natural circumstances, he thought. Perhaps then she would not be so against it. And she may even like him. As I remember him, he is a handsome young man. But I am getting ahead of myself. I must contact his father immediately. Perhaps he is already in love with someone else. And, yes, I could have other young people at the party, young men near her age, as well as a few young women.

Georges Desjardins realized that soon he would be without his Albina. And then he would also lose his precious daughter, Diana. The last years had been a gift to him. She had been a true daughter in every sense of the word. If he could see that she would have a happy life, it would make him feel better about what he must do. It will be only six weeks until her graduation, but the wedding must happen before Albina is taken from him. If she should happen to die before he could arrange a marriage for Diana, the wedding would have to be a simple affair. He must see Albina immediately and tell her of his plan. Georges held his head with his hands. He was suddenly looking his age.

Four Generations—Caroline Tremblay Pichette, Diana Robert Lachance, Marie Louise Pichette Robert, and baby Laurette, 9 months old.

CHAPTER II

Montreal 1915

Diana is now 34 years old. Her children are: Laurette 14, Emilienne (Mimi) 12, Gilberte (Berte) 10, Gerard 6, Germaine 4, Simone 2 and Diana is expecting her seventh child in March of 1916

"The great mischief, the one which destroys our moral existence and threatens the integrity of our mind and our character, is not that we should deceive ourselves and love an uncertain truth, but that we should remain constant to one in which we no longer wholly believe." Maurice Maeterlinck.

Diana was sitting at the dining room table, staring at the magazine that had been placed there, without seeing it. She was trying to focus on what he had said. Her brain felt numb. What was it he had said? That he was leaving? That he was never coming back? No . . . no, that could not be true. She would wake up and find it was something she had dreamed. She glanced at her reflection in the mirror on the dining room wall, not recognizing the face that stared back at her. But at the same time, she was becoming acutely aware of her senses. She was feeling and remembering everything they had gone through together; all of the joys and the worrisome nights when they sat up with sick children, particularly when their dear Marguerite had died. Back then, she didn't think that she could live through the pain she

Gilberte's hand and patted it as she said. "There is something that has happened, but I will explain later when your older sisters and your brother come home. They should be here soon."

"Oh, maman, don't feel sad, everything will be better, you will see." Gilberte hugged her mother as she looked at her face.

"Yes, yes," she said, "I do believe everything will be better." Saying something she was trying to believe, seemed to give Diana hope.

Laughter was coming from the front hall and she recognized her children's voices and knew they were home and hanging up their coats. They burst into the living room laughing as they dropped their books on the dining room table. "It is beautiful out there, maman. The leaves are turning colors, and the air is cool and crisp." Laurette smiled at her mother.

"Are you all right, mam? You look like you don't feel well." Emilienne walked to her mother's side and hugged her. "Are you getting a cold?"

Gerry dumped his books on the dining room table and smiled, "What's for dinner, mam?"

"Our dinner is in the oven. It will be ready soon. Please, all of you come and sit with me. Something has happened that may change our lives, and you need to know. We have many decisions to make, and I want you to understand and help me plan, because we will all be involved and it may not be easy."

Laurette and Emilienne looked at each other with alarm as they quickly picked up Simone and Germaine and held them as they sat around the table. Gilberte and Gerry were seated on each side of their mother. They all looked at her, waiting to hear the news that had made their mother so solemn.

Diana looked at the earnest faces around the table, not knowing how to begin. "I . . . your father was here about three hours ago, and he told me . . . and he told me that he was leaving and never coming back. I . . . I do believe that he will come back one day. I will never give up hope."

"What does he mean, 'never coming back?' Doesn't he love us anymore?" Gilberte asked the question that was in everyone's thoughts. She began to sob, like her heart would break. Then she looked around at the sad faces sitting near her, all of whom looked like they would cry at any moment, and she swallowed hard and started to wipe her tears away. "But . . . but I know he loves us maman. He always told me he did. Why did he go? I don't understand."

"He didn't give any reasons. And I don't want you to stop hoping that he will return. We never suffered when he was here. No matter what anyone tells me, I will never believe that he is a bad man. But the reality is that our way of life will change. I have considered everything since he has been gone. We will have to have food and clothing and enough money to pay rent. I am afraid that with a new baby coming, I will need to stay home to care for the little ones and the new baby. Laurette and Emilienne, I am afraid the burden will fall on your shoulders. You will have to quit school and work. I know that children are employed by several of the clothing designers here in Montreal. Also the glove makers and the furriers hire children. You are both tall and people will think you are older."

Gilberte interrupted, "But maman, don't forget about me. I can do a lot of things and I can sew too. Don't you worry, we will manage."

"My dear girl, you are a petite ten year old. Even the scoundrels who hire children would be afraid to hire one so young and small. You don't appear to be even ten years old."

"But I can tell them I am older. They will listen, when they see what I can do."

"Non, ma petite, non, you are too young. I want you all to know that I will teach you at home. You will never be allowed to speak improper French. I will see that you catch up when you are not working. Some cousins will have books that we can use when they are finished with them, and we will borrow books from the library. I will teach you all every spare moment that we have. And I will teach music lessons at home, and I have assisted Dr. Bujold many times. He told me I have natural skills as a midwife, so I will do everything I can to help us survive and earn what I can. You will have good books to read, and some of the literature that you should all be exposed to. I shall . . . I shall do my best." Diana looked at the concerned young faces around her and tried to sound reassuring.

Both Laurette and Emilienne put down the little girls and they walked over and placed their hands on their mother's shoulders. "We will help, maman. We will do everything we can."

"And don't forget about me, maman. I am almost seven, and I am much more responsible than I used to be. I haven't pounded nails in the windowsills for a long time now, have I mam? Not for years, probably. And I can be a big help to you around the house. You will see that you can depend on me. But I want to know why he left." Gerry looked up at his mother as he spoke, his eyes wet with tears that he kept trying to ignore. "I feel angry and I feel mixed up, and I . . ." he kicked at the leather ottoman near his chair. "Why? Why? I just don't understand it. Were we bad children maman? Did we make him unhappy?"

"No, of course, you did not make him unhappy. And it is natural to feel angry and upset. I don't know why he left. I still think he will return one day, but as I think of all of you, I realize I cannot wait around with any kind of expectation. I have been thinking that I should contact our parish priest, Father Tessier. He has been very kind to us over the years, and maybe he will have some good suggestions about what can be done. I don't know if there is any help for someone like me, but I will find out. Those who could have helped in the past, are dead, and some of my family members are not well off enough to be able to help. But I suppose I should let them know too. But we will manage. Somehow, we will manage."

"What about father's family? Most of them are well off." Laurette looked at her mother as she spoke, her voice sharper than usual. "Don't you think they will want to help when they know what has happened?"

"Perhaps they will, perhaps not. I suppose it depends on how much of a scandal they think it is and how much they want to keep it a secret. Oh, I don't know," Diana had tears in her eyes once more, "I really don't know if they are aware of it, but they may be." She turned and looked at the girls, "Oh, girls, please remove all of your books and finish setting the table. Gilberte started just before you came home. By now the potatoes and the roast are very well done. We should have our dinner."

Emilienne walked to the cupboard. "Let's use our best china, just as if our father were coming home for dinner. And maybe it will make maman feel better."

Laurette joined in the table setting but her thoughts were far away. "I believe what maman said, that she knows he will come back. He is a good man. Wasn't he always patient and kind with us?"

"I know. I always think of him reading the paper to the little ones. I can see them in his arms as he read. I can't forget how he has always helped us with our school-work and given us hints about where we could get useful information."

Laurette was thinking as she worked, recalling their father gently brushing their mother's long wavy hair just a few evenings before. She was remembering everything she thought could be significant, but nothing seemed to make sense. He loved them, she was sure of it.

Diana set the roast and vegetables near the end of the table where she was sitting. She had washed her face and combed her hair. She was smiling when she called all of the children to the table. They looked at her and felt better. They had a beautiful mother, with her large gray eyes and naturally wavy dark hair and light skin. They began to hope that everything would be all right. They bowed their heads as they always had and held hands, while their mother started the blessing. "We thank Thee Lord for all of Thy blessings, and we ask Thy special blessings on this family for we need Thy wisdom and help. Amen."

They ate their dinner in silence; each looking up from the food now and then to smile and reassure their mother as she thoughtfully looked at them. "Does anyone care for apple crisp? I believe it is still warm and I have some whipped cream." Diana spoke in a lighter tone of voice as she smiled at them.

"I do mam, we all do. It smells so good."

Father Tessier had always been a kindly man. Perhaps he would know what to do. Diana and her youngest girls were brought into his office where they waited for him to appear. She busied herself looking at the simple furnishings and the pictures on the wall. She could hear his slow moving footsteps as he approached.

"Bon jour Madame Lachance, and to what do I owe the pleasure of a visit from you? No problems, I hope?"

"I am afraid I have problems, Father, and there seems to be no easy solutions." Diana looked at her gloved hands to keep from crying. "And I hoped you could offer me some advice. You have always been kind and wise. I have no one else to turn to."

"My dear young woman, what has happened?" Father Tessier's ancient face was carved with the painful tasks of his life, his concern for his people and the miseries he had witnessed.

Diana answered slowly, deliberately explaining everything that had happened in great detail. Before she finished, she began to cry. Germaine and Simone stood at her sides hanging on to her skirts as she sat in the chair. Simone started crying and Diana reached down and picked her up. Germaine wanted to be held and also looked on the verge of tears.

"Come to me, Germaine. Your mother does not have the room to hold the two of you." Germaine was used to seeing the old priest and she willingly put up her arms to him. "Tell me Madame Lachance, did you have any indication that his feelings were changing?"

"No, I didn't. He had been absent a lot in the evenings recently and before that he had been gone for some time looking for a new job, but he has been back since June. At times he had some extra work to do and had to work late. But he still seemed himself. He was always kind and loving with the children and me." Diana put Simone down and walked back and forth as she talked. "What can I do? Even simple, fundamental necessities take money for a growing family. I have talked it over with all of the children, and of course, the older girls are willing to work, but I know young girls are paid little and they will have to work so hard. I have always felt that the people who exploit children for their own greed should be stopped, and now I come to this. It is unthinkable, yet, it may be the only answer." She sat down again and picked up Simone who had been close on her heels, "But yet, with six children and a new baby coming, I have no choices. What can I do, Father? In my place, what would you do?"

Father Tessier looked grave. "You must be aware that there are several orphanages. The one I am thinking of is not far from your home. It is staffed by the Sisters of Providence, and most of them are kind young women. I only say most of them because I am not acquainted with all of them."

"But I wouldn't put my children in an orphanage. For one thing, they are not orphans!"

"But they would take the children temporarily, Madame Lachance. Even if the middle children went to the orphanage for a time, it would be two less mouths to feed. What do you think? With the seventh one coming soon, it will be difficult for you to survive."

"I will teach piano lessons, and Dr. Bujold has told me I have natural ability as a midwife. I have assisted him several times in the last months in our own building. I will do anything to keep my family together; don't you understand? They are my children and they are my responsibility, and I love and need them as much as they need me. And perhaps, if we are lucky, my husband will get over whatever is . . . is . . . driving him and he will return. You know, Father Tessier, since he has left I have had a lot of time to wonder if my strict convent education truly prepared me for the parts of marriage that are so private between a man and a woman. That was never explained to me and I thought if I loved him enough, that it would mean everything to him. But I was aware when I married Gaudiose that he was always attracted to women, and many women were attracted to him. I was very happy in the life we shared together and he told me we were the reasons his life had meaning." She hesitated for a moment and looked at the old priest. "Though he seemed disappointed when I told him I was pregnant with another child. Though those thoughts never seemed to enter his head when we made love. Those are the things my marriage has taught me. Apparently, I become pregnant easily. Somehow, I can't believe what many have suggested, that he did not want the responsibility of a family. But yet, I will never give up hoping he will return. I know in my heart I shall always love him. Though during my anxious moments at night when I think of what the children will have to go through, I feel so frustrated and I feel such anger at him for putting the children through that. I am an adult and I should be able to take anything . . . but the children . . . it is so difficult for them. God forgive me for my thoughts." Diana had risen from her chair during the long conversation still hanging on to Simone. She turned back as she spoke. "I am sorry to have bothered you for so long with my personal troubles. I did not know I could tell anyone all of these private things. But somehow it helped me to speak of it."

"Do not worry about that my child. I am a very old man, and I have heard everything. You have courage, and I believe you will manage. "Father Tessier looked suddenly lifeless and old.

"That is the only suggestion you have, the orphanage? Somehow, I had hoped there could be another answer. I have been making inquiries and I know the government has no laws to help widows and abandoned families. But I can't thank you enough for allowing me to talk. It helped me just to be able to speak freely about it with you." She took Germaine by the hand and she carried Simone. The pram stood outside the office door.

Father Tessier stood in the doorway to his office and stopped Diana before she left. "The St. Vincent de Paul Society does do some things to help the poor. I don't believe it is much and I believe you must apply for it, but you should look into it. I know there is nothing else available. And they might be able to help in an emergency."

"Thank you, Father, for remembering that. One never knows. I will take my girls and look into it tomorrow. It is good to be able to hope."

Diana hurried along the streets with her girls. It was time for the older girls and Gerry to be home from school. She pulled the pram up the steps to the door, and left it in the front hall. The girls and Gerry were sitting around the dining room table when she entered the apartment.

"Maman, we have news. Good news! We spoke to Sister Mary James and we told her we may need to find work and she told us of a factory that makes hand made leather gloves, and they hire girls our age! She asked us if we could sew and we told her we all could sew. She said she has a niece that works there, but that she works long hours for not much money. But mam, it would be a start!"

"That is wonderful news girls, but I want you to finish the school year. It is about two and a half months till the Christmas break; then you can begin. We can manage our finances till then. But thank you, thank you. I don't know what I would do without you. One thing more, I did let the other residents know that I would be teaching piano and I now have four piano students in our building. They will be weekly students and it will not pay a lot, but every bit will help."

"Oh, mam," Gerry ran to his mother and hugged her, "maybe everything is going to be all right. I was so afraid when you said papa had left. I knew about a boy at school whose father left them, and he has not been in school for a long time, and I heard today that he and the other children in his family are at an orphanage."

"We will all try to stay together, Gerry." Diana was reminded of what Father Tessier had advised her to do, but she kept it to herself.

"Maman, did you see Father Tessier today?" Emilienne asked. "Did he have any suggestions that could help us?"

"No, not a thing, at least nothing that I will even consider now." Diana drew closer to Emilienne. "He actually mentioned the orphanage as a temporary solution, but I will never consider it, unless it means survival for any of you. And I believe we should start looking for an inexpensive apartment. Our place here is just more than we will be able to pay, under these circumstances."

Emilienne put her arms around her mother. "I know we have to be strong. But mam, it is going to be difficult isn't it?"

"Yes, it will. I think none of us can imagine what it will be like. We have been sheltered from a lot of things in our lives and we have been fortunate. But I am going to get as much help as I can so we can stay together." Diana's look reassured her daughter.

Gilberte had been looking very preoccupied. "Maman, I have been doing a lot of thinking since papa left. Last week when I was walking home from school, I saw papa with a lady and he went into her house. I started to say hello but he didn't see me. I wondered if we went to that house if he would be there. Maybe he would come home with us. Do you think so mam?"

Diana looked stricken, but she knew from looking at Gilberte that she was very serious. "My darling girl, are you quite sure that you saw your father?"

"Yes, maman. I walk that way every day."

"We can talk about this later, Gilberte. I think it is time we have some dinner. Would you girls help set the table? We are having leftovers tonight so it won't take long to prepare."

After the dinner dishes were cleared away and washed, the children were either at the dining room table doing their school work, or they were seated at chairs in the living room catching up on their reading. Diana was busy crocheting a bonnet for the new baby, when she put down her work and got up and walked over to where Gilberte was reading.

"Do you think you could find the house where you saw your father?" Diana's voice quivered as she asked.

"Yes, maman, I know the house. It is on the street near here. It is made of stone, but it has an outside stairway. It is Delorimier Street," replied Gilberte.

"I have been thinking of what you have said. Maybe it is not too late. Will you show me the house?" Diana spoke quietly so as not to disturb the other children.

"Yes, maman, it is still light out, so I know I can find it. We can go now, before it is dark."

Diana took Gilberte by the hand as they hurried along the

street. It would be dark soon so they must walk fast. Diana did not say anything as they walked along. Her mind relived the scene of his departure. At the time, she was shocked and sat in mute silence, wondering if she had heard the words he had spoken. Thinking back on it now, it all seemed so quick, so deadly and final. If only he had shouted and accused her of something . . . something she could have answered that would have given her a chance to fight back, because it had been unjust, but only the cold announcement of his departure still felt unreal.

As they approached the house, Gilberte pointed it out to her mother. They walked up the metal steps and stood in front of the door. Diana peeked into the oval shaped window. The door opened into a foyer, but she could see a dark haired man speaking to a woman sitting at a table in the next room. She knocked on the door as loudly as she could, while she kept her eyes on the man at the table. He looked up and started for the door. She could see that it was her husband. She called out, "Please don't do this, please don't do this, Gaudiose." He stopped, then looked as if he would unlock the door, then backed away, turned and walked into the room and was suddenly out of sight.

Diana sank down on the steps like a deflated balloon. Her knees had given way and she was shaking all over, her eyes swimming with tears. Muffled sobs seemed to come from her throat. Gilberte sat on the steps and held her mother's hand, her own tears streaming down her cheeks. "I am so sorry maman. Papa must be sick, otherwise he would never leave us."

Diana shivered all of the way back. Gilberte's hand was still in her mother's and she felt her mother tremble as they walked home. She knew it wasn't cold out, and she worried about her mother and the baby she was carrying. Her own heart felt large like it had expanded and would break inside. But she knew that her mother was walking blindly, not seeing the street ahead, and she must remain strong for her. She would take her home so she could put her maman into bed where she would feel warm and safe. She wondered if any of them would ever feel safe again.

Diana remained in bed for the next few days. She looked so

pale and she seemed to stare at nothing. Her lifeless look had frightened Gilberte and she did not want to leave her. She had insisted her older sisters and her brother finish school as their mother desired. She would go back when her mother was stronger.

One afternoon, she went to the neighbors who had a telephone and called Dr. Bujold's office. She told him her mother was not well, and he should come because she needed his advice. Gilberte liked Dr. Bujold. Hadn't he been there to attend to her mother when she gave birth all seven times? She trusted him. She would tell him of their problems and maybe he would know what kind of medicine her mother needed.

When Dr. Bujold arrived, Gilberte told him in her own way what had happened. He asked her a few questions, questions she answered honestly, and simply. He spent some time with Diana talking calmly to her as he examined her. When there was no response, he spoke sharply. "Hiding yourself away like this will do you no good, Diana. Your children need you to be strong. You must take care of yourself for your own sake and for your family. Now this is enough." His voice grew sharper and louder. Diana blinked. Life seemed to be coming back into her eyes and face. She looked around.

"Gilberte, have I been ill?"

"Yes, maman."

She tried to sit up. "How long have I been in bed? When did you arrive, Dr. Bujold?"

"I think that you have been in bed for three days, pale and unresponsive. Gilberte called me. She thought you needed some medicine."

"Did she tell you what has happened?"

"She did and my dear young woman, I won't minimize your problems, but other women have gone through similar times and they pulled through. You and I must put our heads together and see what can be done. You don't have time to be ill." Then Dr. Bujold looked directly at Gilberte. "Do you have a tin of broth or any kind of soup in the house that you could prepare for your mother? She should eat something. She needs her strength."

"I think we have some food left. I will look." Gilberte ran back into the kitchen and disappeared into the pantry.

Dr. Bujold turned his attention back to Diana. "How much money do you have and how long can you survive, given your expenses every month?"

Diana looked on Dr. Bujold as a long time family friend. She was surprised by his question, but she realized his interest was in her welfare and the welfare of her children.

Diana's eyes filled with tears, "To answer your question, our money may last for six weeks if we are careful. I had hoped it would stretch till after Christmas, but now I know there is no hope of that. We had some savings, but when I checked at the bank so I could plan exactly how long before the children would have to work, I was shocked, but it has vanished."

"I understand that you have not notified any family of your troubles."

"No, I haven't. I would like to, but I don't want to make them feel like I expect them to help. My sisters are not well off. They get by, and they have good husbands who take care of them."

"What about your husband's people? Certainly they will not stand by and see you and your children suffer."

"I am not sure. They are a proud family. They will not want anyone to know of it and a scandal like this . . . they will not want to hear of it."

"But surely . . ."

Diana looked down, averting her eyes from his, "I . . . I feel like a failure. I can't look at myself without feeling, I somehow, didn't make my husband happy. I feel worthless, and what can I tell them about what happened? I have gone over everything in my mind many times. Perhaps I am unsophisticated in what a man expects, but I honestly don't know why he felt the need for other women. I believed we had a beautiful life. We loved each other and I believed we were happy."

Gilberte was carrying a steaming bowl of broth. "Maman, I made you some broth and some bread with butter. I think it will make you feel stronger." She turned to Dr. Bujold after she set the tray down on the bedside table. "Will that be enough for her?"

"Yes, that will be sufficient for now, Gilberte. You are a young lady of many talents." Dr. Bujold smiled at them.

"Diana, I am afraid I have to go. Madame Gautier is expecting a baby to arrive any time, and I am on my way there now, but I will think further on your problem. You are still suffering from shock, but your children need you and it is up to you to be strong. They will not survive without you."

"Thank you for coming, Doctor Bujold. You helped me more than you know." Diana turned to Gilberte who had been standing by waiting to see if her mother needed anything else. "And my dear girl, thank you always for caring so much."

Gilberte went back to school, and the last days seemed to go quickly. The money was quickly running out and the older girls would soon be working. They had learned of many manufacturers that hired children.

Diana finally decided to visit her sisters and tell them of her plight. She and her three sisters, Albina, Florina, and Cecile, were all seated at the kitchen table, which was always the most popular room in Albina's house. Yellow curtains and yellow and blue walls and a long table to accommodate a large family made up the kitchen. She was surprised to learn how shocked they seemed when she told them what happened.

"You don't come often. I knew something must be wrong when you wrote that you were coming. But this . . . I never dreamed such a thing could happen to you. Your husband is an educated man. You are educated. Circumstances like this don't seem to happen to people like you." Albina stood up and took the tea pot from the stove and poured them all more tea while she looked directly at Diana.

"I am not sure just how to take that, Albina. Am I so different than you?"

"No, of course not. It is just that our uncle saw that you had a very special education. You were his favorite and he wanted to do something for you. We went to a convent school also, but it was not on a par with the schooling and the refinements you were exposed to."

"I was only four when that was all decided for me. I didn't ask for it, nor did I want it. And as a matter of fact, I was a very lonely child. I was too young to be at a boarding school and away from all of you."

"Albina just means that we didn't expect that you would ever be facing this kind of trouble." Florina looked concerned and sympathetic as she spoke to Diana.

"I can't say that it hasn't been a shock for me too," Diana blinked back the tears that were so close to spilling out. She stood up. "I came to let you know. At this point, I am not sure what I can do. The older girls will have to work and I will do all I can . . . but the babies will need me at home."

Diana thought about the conversation she had with her sisters as she rode home on the street car. She knew they were sympathetic, and would help, if it came to that. But they had little and she did not want to be a taker. Cecile hadn't said a word, but her eyes had filled with tears. My sisters are good, but what can they do, she thought.

All avenues of potential help seemed to Diana to be closing off. She was still undecided about whether or not she should go to her husband's family. They had never been unkind to her, but she remembered once being called frivolous because she took her older children to an opera matinee. She had taught them all of the words to the major arias of Carmen and they were familiar with the story, so she thought they must see it. She had purchased the least expensive tickets that had cost only pennies, and they sat in the top row in the uppermost balcony. She had always felt that learning to love music should be part of their lives. Perhaps she had been frivolous. Perhaps she should have insisted on a less expensive apartment, when Gaudiose had found it, and cut way down on food expenses. Gaudiose had always told her what a good cook she was and she had tried so hard to please him. Somewhere, somehow, she had done the unforgivable. What it had been, she didn't know. She may never know. Or Gaudiose was in trouble, or perhaps he was in love with another woman. After all, he had been gone for a long time when he was looking for a new job. Or he may just be tired of the responsibility. Could it possibly have been that? It was true that Gaudiose wasn't in favor of more children, and was disappointed when she told him she was pregnant again. That had hurt her because she had loved him so much. He had been the one who had wanted to make love, and she knew her duty as a wife, and he had been gone so long. Wasn't it a wife's duty to respond to a husband's request? It had been a joy and a pain when she found she was pregnant, remembering what Gaudiose had said. Suddenly she was aware that the streetcar was approaching her street.

The day came when Laurette and Emilienne were going to start their first day of work. Laurette would be sewing in the suits and coats section of a clothing manufacturer. It would be straight seams of specific sections of a coat. Emilienne was starting at a hand made glove manufacturer across the street from where Laurette would work. She would be sewing leather gloves by hand. The girls were excited about it.

It was only when they were on the streetcar early in the morning that they realized how their lives would be changed. "Do you realize that we are now adults, Emilienne? Are you nervous about it? I feel a little scared, and excited too."

"No Laurette, I am not nervous about it, but I do worry that I will be able to do the kind of work that will satisfy them. I have heard that sewing gloves all day is difficult work." Emilienne looked at her gloved hands and inspected them as she spoke.

"Yes, I imagine sewing through leather and using such small precise stitches will be difficult. But I think God will help us. He knows we will work hard and he will help us to do well." Laurette looked so serious as she spoke.

"What you will be doing will be precise too, and sewing in heavy materials is hard and heavy work. I suppose what you said about being adults is almost true. Somehow I feel older, and I am sure we will learn all about life and hard work and people.

But tell me Laurette, we will be there for twelve hours. What did you make for yourself for lunch today?"

"I never thought about how many hours we would be there. I just fixed a piece of buttered bread and an apple. What did you make?"

Emilienne laughed out loud. "Why, I happened to choose the same thing!" Her face was serious once more. "Because I didn't want to take anything that maman might want to use for our dinner this evening. I know she is trying hard to make the food last longer."

"My reasons, precisely. I have a feeling we will be hungry before we are home tonight. They both laughed again. And when they looked at each other, they could see tears in their eyes. They put their arms around each other and clung for a few minutes. Laurette looked up. "We are almost there, my dear sister, bon chance!"

"Bon chance and be brave! I will meet you here after work." They jumped off the streetcar and ran in opposite directions.

Diana had made a point of discussing their change of fortune with the landlord, Monsieur La Beau. He and his wife had been kind in the past and she hoped they would have ideas of where she could go with her family to find an apartment that would be much less expensive. At first they insisted she stay, saying that perhaps her fortunes would change. But she was determined that they must leave, knowing her finances would never be sufficient under the present circumstances, and it would be dishonest to allow them to believe otherwise. They then suggested that a relative had an apartment house in another area of east Montreal and that the apartment would be less than half of the price. Diana asked, "Are there schools and parks in the neighborhood?"

"Why, yes, there are. All within a few blocks."

"It sounds like it would be good for children. If you would be kind enough to write down the address for me and the name of the landlord, I would be very much obliged."

Monsieur La Beau took a small notebook out of his pocket and began jotting down the address. He looked up briefly while he was writing and said, "I wanted you to be aware that the apartment is in a poor neighborhood."

"Yes, yes of course. I understand that it will not be a neighborhood like this. As long as you can assure me it is safe, and it is within my limited budget, I shall be happy to have it."

"Yes, to my knowledge, it is a safe neighborhood. There are many children there. I just didn't know what you were expecting."

Gilberte and Gerry had gone to the market for their mother. When they returned with their arms filled with groceries, they were excited to learn about their sisters. "I am sorry we spent all of the fifty three cents you gave us maman. But we did get everything you wanted: the potatoes, the onions, the carrots and the bread. And maman, I have been excited all day thinking about Laurette and Emilienne. Are they home from work yet? I was thinking they would be home now. I am so anxious to hear about their work and how they liked it."

"No, they will not be finished with their work till 7:00 this evening. I don't think they took very much for their lunches and they will be hungry when they get back. They left at six this morning, and it will be eight before they are back. Our dinner is in the oven, so we can eat soon if you would like. Or we can wait till the girls are home."

"Oh maman, we would like to wait for the girls. We are so excited for them."

"We were worried about Laurette and Emilienne, mam. We didn't know it would be such a long day. I hope they aren't too tired." Gerry looked up at his mother, his eyes betraying his troubled thoughts.

"I am sure they are fine. But you are right: they will be very tired. You seem troubled, Gerry."

"I still get a stomach ache when I think of papa, mam. I feel angry at him. And I feel that way a lot. Why did he do it, maman?" Gerry began sobbing as he ran to his mother. "How could he love us one day, and leave us the next? I hate him, I hate him, mam." He cried harder, as if every tear had been wrung out of him. He continued to cry as he talked. "No, no, I don't really hate him. I love him, that's why I want him . . . that's why I want him back."

Diana reached for her son. She put her arms around him and hugged him to her, cupping his head in her hand, her face close to his. She spoke softly, "I don't know why he left, but I know it has nothing to do with his love for you or your sisters. He has loved all of you and I am sure he continues to love you today. We can only guess at his reasons and perhaps one day we will all understand." She took a clean handkerchief out of her pocket and wiped his nose and eyes, dabbing at her own eyes before she put it back into her pocket.

Gilberte's eyes were wet as she watched her brother. "Gerry and I can set the table, mam. You will help me won't you Gerry? Perhaps the little ones should eat now. They are young and they are always hungry."

Gilberte Lachance, 15 years old

CHAPTER III

Gilberte's Voice

"Ordinarily one learns from experience the necessity of modifying our wishful thinking to conform to the realities of existence; to change from thinking on the basis of the pleasure principle to thinking on the basis of the reality principle, as Freud put it." Dr. Karl A. Menninger   The Human Mind

I never thought it would come to this. My maman is still trying to keep us all together, but with the new baby, the money that Laurette and Emilienne earn never seems quite enough for all of the food we need. Something happened to my mother's milk. Dr. Bujold said he thought it was stress, and that is why it stopped coming. My new sister is a beautiful baby and a good baby, but she cries a lot. Maman said it is because she is often hungry. Maman tried a formula that Dr. Bujold suggested, made out of cow's milk, but it seems to give her pains. I keep asking maman to let me work, but she said I am still too young. I am eleven years old now and I want to help. My brother Gerry and I said we would go to the orphanage if it would make things easier, but maman refuses to allow it. I hear her crying at night and it makes me cry too, because I know she is sad. She still says our father will come home soon and he still loves us.

My sister Laurette and Emilienne are still working at the same jobs. They come home every night looking more and more tired. They don't tell us they are tired and they don't complain, but I think it is harder than they want us to believe. At first they seemed to talk a lot about everything that happened. Some things were funny and they made us laugh, and they laughed with us, but now they don't talk at all. They eat their supper and go to bed. My maman looks at them with tears in her eyes and she looks away so we won't notice.

Maman has two new piano students and two of the students she had when we lived in our other apartment. Our new apartment is not as nice, but what is important is that we are together. The rooms are smaller and some of the windows don't close tightly, but we are managing quite well. The people here seem to be polite. We don't know anyone yet. Many of them seem to have sad faces, and when I asked my maman why it was, she said that life had not been kind to them.

We have a telephone in our apartment building. Very few people have them. It is in the foyer of the building and it may be used for emergencies. Last week we had an emergency. Mrs. O'Brien who was new in our building, was expecting a baby at any time. Mrs. O'Brien has seven other children and she didn't know a doctor in Montreal. Maman guessed that she didn't have money for a doctor. So when Maman heard she was in trouble, she called Dr. Bujold, who couldn't come, but he told my mother what to do. She did it and when there were more problems, I called Dr. Bujold again and took his message to mam. She has strong hands and she was able to turn the baby and it was born without any more problems. Everyone in the building was waiting outside of the apartment in the hallway. When they heard the baby cry, they cheered.

Mr. O'Brien cried when my maman told him his wife was going to be just fine and he had a healthy baby girl. I guess I forgot to say that he had seven sons. I helped my maman take home all of the bloody linens and towels and we washed them and brought them back clean and ironed. Mr.O'Brien, who is a butcher, brought my maman enough meat to last for two weeks and eight liters of milk. She thanked him and I could tell she was happy.

Maman seems happier since she helped Mrs. O'Brien. She said people smile at her in the hallways of the building. She doesn't speak their language and they don't speak hers, but they all show kindness to her and seem willing to help. There are two other French families in the building, and the others are from other places in the world. I think she does not feel so alone.

Today is the day that Gerry and I will take a street car to the orphanage to see what it is like. We have been talking about it a lot. We don't want to go there, but if it helps maman, we decided we would see it, and tell her about it, and it might help her to decide what to do.

We were both a little scared when we stopped in front of the old gray stone building. It is called Providence Orphanage. The brass door knocker on the heavy carved door, was huge. When I lifted it and let it drop, the harsh sound seemed to echo down the street. At that moment, I wanted to run away, and I hoped no one would answer. A small window in the upper half of the door opened and a nun's face looked out at us. "Whom do you wish to visit?"

Gerry surprised me and said, "My friend David La Fontaine, please."

"And who are you?"

"My name is Gerard Lachance and this is my sister, Gilberte. David La Fontaine was in my school."

"Come in. I will see if he is working or if he can see you. The children here have tasks to do every day before they go to classes or may have visitors. Please wait here. I will be back in a few minutes." Her shoes sounded hard on the stone floor and seemed to echo in the cavernous foyer.

I looked up and was fascinated by the stairway that came down into the center of the large room. The stairway went up four floors, with a landing on each floor. On the top floor the ceiling was a large dome of stained glass, very much like one I have seen in an old church. There were balconies on every floor that surrounded the central staircase, with doors all around. I looked at Gerry and asked, "What made you decide to mention your friend?"

FAMILY VOICES

"I didn't plan to, but I just remembered that this is where he went about five months ago. And I haven't seen him since he left school."

"I think it was a good idea. It will give us a chance to talk to someone who is actually living here. Oh, Sister is coming back."

"He is almost finished with his work, so he may see you for a few minutes. Follow me please."

Gerry and I followed the nun to a large room off of the foyer. David was sitting at a large table polishing brass candlesticks. When he saw Gerry, he got up and ran to him. Gerry hugged him and said, "How are you David? This is my sister, Gilberte. We wanted to see how you are doing."

David looked at the nun rather shyly, and she spoke. "I will be back in ten minutes, David, and you can complete your work then."

"Thank you, Sister." Then he looked at Gerry and me as she walked out of the room. "Why, I am doing all right. It is not the best place in the world, but we are surviving."

"Would you choose to come here if you had a choice?" I couldn't help but ask the question that was in my mind.

David looked around nervously. "No, of course not. No one would."

"Why?"

"When my father left, my mother had no choice. I guess that is the part I don't like. I don't like not knowing how they are managing. I am the oldest and we have many others. Three other sisters are here, and the two youngest ones are home with my mother. I don't know how they are eating and existing."

"Didn't your mother have any family to help?" Gilberte asked.

"She does, but they are poor, and she does not want to ask them for help."

"How is the food, David? You look like you are not eating much." Gerry looked concerned.

"At first, I was hungry all of the time, but I am getting used to eating less. The food is okay, what there is of it. We don't have meat. We sometimes have a little butter. I shouldn't complain." David paused for a minute, gathering his thoughts. "Actually, the nuns here are kind and they do a lot of good for people with what they have. They do not eat anything different than we all do, and really not any more than we do. It sounds like Sister Marie Therese is coming back. I am happy you came. I haven't seen any of my friends for a long time. Thank you for coming."

Gerry looked thoughtful. "You never know, maybe we will be back. It was good to see you, David."

* * *

My second day at the orphanage helped me to realize that we had led a sheltered life. Sister Marie Therese asked me to help her with some new children who had just arrived. Their father had brought them in saying that he could not cope with them any longer. His wife had died in child-birth and he had tried to keep them together, but now he had no work. The children were dirty and hungry. Their heads were infested with lice and the youngest girls and the baby needed some special care.

Sister showed me how to sew flannel bonnets and night gowns for them. I helped to hold them while Sister shaved their heads. We bathed them and loosened the scabs on their heads, which were filled with nits, or lice eggs. Sister knew what to do for them, and she put a soothing ointment on them so it would not be painful. She asked that I stay with them so they would not be frightened, and they seemed happy that I would be with them. The baby was nine months old and the girls were two and three. It made me think of my own three little sisters, so I was happy they were not afraid. When I heard the little girls talking to each other during the night, it made me feel good that we had been able to help them. The two year old, Lisa said, "Katie, does your head feel good? Mine feels nice. I like my hat. My head is warm and it doesn't hurt any more."

"My head feels good too. Sister said when our hair grows out, our heads will be healed, and the other children won't know we don't have any hair while we are wearing our bonnets. Wasn't that a good idea?"

"She is kind, and I like Gilberte too. I am not afraid any more. Our baby sister hasn't been crying at all. She drank a big bottle of milk, and now she is sleeping."

I wondered if there was enough milk for my baby sister Cecile and if she was peacefully asleep with a full tummy. There never seemed to be enough food when I was home, and rarely enough milk for Cecile. She had to have it. My head seemed to be so full of thoughts: it was hard to sleep. The narrow cot that Sister had given me was hard and I could feel the springs. I kept wondering what would happen next. As long as I could help, and there would be one less mouth to feed at home, I would stay. When maman thought I was old enough to work, I would go home. I missed my family already. I am glad Gerry stayed at home. Maman thought he was too young, and I wondered what he would have done surrounded by strangers.

The next morning Sister Marie Therese and Mother Marie Pierre came to our room to see how we did. I was helping the little girls into their clothes. Mother Marie Pierre spoke to me first. "Sister Marie Therese tells me that you are a very mature eleven year old. I wondered if you would mind staying with Gabrielle Letourneau. She has not been well and we don't have enough staff to attend to her needs."

"I would be happy to help if I could. Has she had a doctor?"

"She has had a bad cold that does not seem to go away. At times she is feverish. The doctor comes here when he has time. He is overworked but he helps out when he can."

"Will Lisa and Katie and their baby sister be all right alone? I don't want them to be afraid."

"I will put one of their older sisters in with them. They won't be afraid. And thank you Gilberte. Thank you, for doing such a good job with them." Sister Marie Therese took my hand and smiled.

"They are sweet children. They remind me of my baby sisters at home. But if I can help, I'll be happy."

Gabrielle Letourneau's room was at the end of the long corridor on the first floor. I was told it was the isolation room in the event the child may have had something contagious. The room smelled of sickness and was cold and damp. The gray stone walls were cold to the touch and the window was cracked, with old newspapers stuck in it. A small girl was coughing on the cot in the corner. She may have been six or seven years old. I could see her red hair on the pillow as I walked closer. "Gabrielle? My name is Gilberte Lachance. I am going to be staying with you. I will see if we can make your cold better. What have you eaten today?"

"I couldn't eat much. It comes up, I cough so hard."

"You need to eat so you can get well. Do you ever go out?"

"No, I haven't been out for a long time, months, I think. I have been so weak. It is hard to walk."

"I am going to see if I can find something for you to eat. I will be back as soon as I can."

Sister Marie Therese was walking down the hall so I ran to catch up to her. "Sister, the room is too damp and cold for Gabrielle. Oh Sister, I am afraid for her. I need to get her something to eat. She doesn't eat and she is so feverish. Sister, I think she is very sick . . . Could we get her some broth?"

"We'll try, Gilberte. Come with me first while I check the room. I have not seen Gabrielle for a time. The girl who was looking after her, left yesterday. I didn't know she had gotten worse."

"I am scared, Sister. Even her eyes look sick. And she is so thin."

"Don't worry, we will take care of her."

As we walked into the room, I could hear Sister Marie Therese take in her breath. She didn't say anything, but she walked to the window and looked angry. She touched Gabrielle who was coughing, and took me by the hand and walked out.

I looked at her, and though I wasn't sure, she seemed angry. "Are you angry with me?"

"No, I am not. I am just wondering why it took so long for someone to have noticed how sick she is. Gabrielle needs help. She needs to be in the hospital. Would you mind staying with her tonight? I will see what we can arrange for her tomorrow, and now we must find her some broth."

Gabrielle drank the broth we brought her. She smiled at me. "Gilberte, I am so happy you are with me. I don't like to be alone. I feel better knowing you are here." But as the day wore on, her coughing became worse. Her thin face was pale, and her eyes were glazed. She kept saying she was cold. She couldn't get warm. I gave her the blanket that was on my cot. But she was still cold. I didn't know what to do. I ran down the hall to see if anyone was still up, but everything was quiet. So I went quietly back to her. "Don't go Gilberte. Please . . . please don't leave me again. I'm afraid."

"I am not going anywhere. If you don't get warm soon, I am going to crawl into bed with you and try to keep you warm. I remember going into bed with my mother when I was very young or sick and my mother had a way of holding me close. She would lie on her side and pull her knees into a chair like position, and I would move my back against her tummy, like I was sitting on her lap, and she would put her arms around me and I would stop trembling and I would soon be warm. Do you know what I mean?"

"Yes, yes, I remember my mother holding me like that before she died. Yes, she kept me warm that way. I would like that."

Gabrielle coughed most of the night and I whispered to her to relax, and I gave her some water to drink. The coughing continued until it was almost light, and then she slept. And I must have slept too, for after awhile, my arm that was under her body felt numb and she felt cool.

When I awoke, I felt stiff and I tried to move my arms and change positions, but I did not want to awaken her. She had such a terrible night.

There was a soft knock at the door. "Anyone awake yet?" Sr. Marie Therese stepped into the room and noticed where I was sleeping. "Did you sleep with her, Gilberte?"

"Yes, Sister I did. She couldn't get warm and she was coughing so much, I held her to help her to stop shivering and coughing and go to sleep. My maman used to hold me like this when I was little when I was afraid or cold."

"Thank you, Gilberte. You did what was needed to help her sleep."

"Sister, she is sleeping so well that I hate to move and wake her. She was awake most of the night, coughing." I whispered as I spoke to her, "But my arm is numb." I moved quietly, pulled my arm out from under her and slipped out of the bed. "I am surprised she is still asleep, but she is cooler."

Sister Marie Therese put her hand on Gabrielle's head. She picked up her hand and held it for awhile, then placed it under the blanket. She had a concerned look on her face.

"Did I do all right? I didn't know what else to do."

"You did just fine. You probably gave her the most comfort that she has known in a long time. I . . . I hesitate to tell you this, but Gabrielle is dead. She is with the angels in heaven." Sister had tears in her eyes.

"But she can't be dead, she just can't be, I held her so nothing bad would happen. She can't be dead. She can't be . . ." I began to cry.

"I know you did everything possible, and I know she loved having you close." Sister Marie Therese put her arms around me. "Oh, my dear girl, we don't know why these things happen. In fact . . . yes . . . I do know why these things happen. It is the poverty that we are all afflicted with, the lack of available doctors and nursing care to help. I joined this order and I love being a nun, but so often I am frustrated by our lack of financial resources that could help." Sister Marie Therese began to cry, as she held me close, then she wiped her eyes and said, "I am so sorry, you sweet girl, I should not be talking like this. Forgive me. I should tell Mother Marie Pierre that Gabrielle has died. Come with me, Gilberte. We will go to her together. She will probably ask you what kind of night Gabrielle had, and just tell her like you told me. She is an overworked woman who never has enough time, but she will be understanding."

FAMILY VOICES

Laurette Lachance in a dress she designed and made.

CHAPTER IV

Laurette's Voice

"Do not be greedy of consolation. I never got anything that way. Suffering teaches: Life teaches."

Baron Friedrich von Hugel   Letters from Baron Friedrich von Hugel to a neice

I am happy maman doesn't really know what our days are like. She would be even more depressed than she is now. I think I have never been so tired in my life. I can't seem to catch up on rest. There are not enough hours in the day to catch up. One does not have to think to do a job like I have. Oh, I must be careful, and the materials are very heavy, but after a time it is such a routine that my mind can focus on happier times while I am sewing. It makes the hours in the day go faster.

Mr. McDermott, the foreman on our floor, has been following me around lately. He has told me I am a "pretty little thing." I pretend I don't hear him. At first when he was nice to me, I thought he was just being kind. Now I worry that he has other things on his mind, because his actions are telling me so. Sometimes he rubs up against me when he walks by. Other times he blows on the back of my neck when I am bent over the machine. It is getting more difficult to ignore him. I would like to talk to his boss, but I am afraid if I complain, I won't keep this job long. And most jobs require a period of training time during which I wouldn't make any money. I don't think we could manage at home without my pay. So I try to avoid him when I must go to pick up my boxes of cut materials to begin my day.

I really haven't had any time to know some of the other girls who work here. They do as we all do. After work they run for the streetcar and go home where they eat their supper and go to bed, just as Mimi and I have for over a year now.

We have twenty minutes for lunch. If we had more time it would be nice to have a picnic outdoors in the sunshine. I would love that. We do have Sundays off, but there is always so much of everything to catch up on. Maman always wants us to read or study. She feels so sad that often we are too tired to do anything except have time with our brother and sisters. But there is always housework, and sometimes I don't feel like doing it, but somehow, it is so different from my job that it is a pleasant relief for me. We all share in the work, and it seems more like play. And just being with family is good for me. I miss seeing the little ones. They seem to be growing so fast. They will not be babies for many more years.

I love to cook, and maman seems to think I will be a good one. I enjoy doing meat when we happen to have it. And maman often lets me do our Sunday dinner. We can't often afford meat, but now she is getting to know the butcher in our new neighborhood, and he lets her know when he has special sales. Mam has taught me how to make a wonderful kidney pie. Kidneys are usually the least expensive meat of all, though sometimes a pound of mutton or veal is twelve cents a pound, so occasionally we have a treat even if it is a stew with vegetables and a bit of meat. There are many of us so it does not go far.

At times I cry because I miss our father. I think what he did to our mother was bad, but I still love him and will always think he was wonderful while he was with us. But I don't understand how a man like he is could leave us. Somehow the two things in his personality don't fit. He is kind on one hand, and on the other hand he probably did not want the responsibility. Maman does not want us to speak badly of our father. She always says that they were both young when they were married, and perhaps he wasn't ready for the responsibilities of a large family.

The only words I overheard him speak to my mother in anger were when he said he did not want more children. I could see tears forming in my mother's eyes. I know she felt terrible. She tried so hard to please him. She is so religious.

It seems, at times, that the only comforting words she gets now are from our old parish priest who has much difficulty walking. He stops to see how we are managing sometimes. Maman thinks he is more than ninety years old and she says she knows he has had a hard life. She said he worked in the missions in Africa when he was young. She often asks him if he would like to stay for a meal. But he always gives her the same answer, "No, you give it to your children." I often notice the pain in his eyes when he looks at Cecile. She looks too thin for her age. The rest of us are thin too, and now that Gilberte is at the orphanage, I can hardly stand it. She shouldn't be there. The last time I could visit her, her eyes seemed so enormous with dark circles around them. I want her to come home. I know in her mind, she went there to help us. She told me before she left, there would be one less mouth to feed, and when maman would allow her to work, she would come home. I could see that she is not eating much where she is. And now it has been almost a year. I am going to tell maman to bring Gilberte home. She can probably find work sewing at a designer's boutique. In fact, I'm sure she could. She has spent most of her life, designing clothes for everyone of us and telling us all how to dress. It makes me smile to think of it. Though, I don't want her to work twelve hours a day. She wouldn't last long. It would kill her. Though the way she looks now, she looks like she gets very little rest. Maybe she is too willing to help.

I told maman that she should go and see Gilberte today and that Mimi and I would take care of the children. I know she will feel that she must bring Gilberte home when she sees how thin she is.

Gerard Lachance

CHAPTER V

Gerard's Voice

"But how entirely I live in my imagination; how completely depend upon spurts of thought, coming as I walk, as I sit; things churning up in my mind and so making a perpetual pageant, which is to be my happiness." Virginia Woolf, A Writer's Diary

I often take the long walk home after school so I can walk by the St. Lawrence River and see the red sumac trees in the fall. The red sumac and the green of the pines make me feel good inside. I love to watch the ice islands floating down the river in the spring when everything is melting. I like to pretend I am riding on one and I am off on a great trip of exploration. But most of all, it also gives me the excuse to walk by the stables where Monsieur Renaud's horses are kept. The stables are old and built of stone, and are not far from La Gauchetiere St. where we live. The best part is that the horses know me now and they come close to say hello. I whisper in their ears, and I hug them. And I always pat their noses and their necks because they seem to like it. One day after school when I stopped, I was talking with the horses and brushing Figarro's coat when Msr. Renaud stopped by.

"You're young Lachance, aren't you?"

"Yes sir, I am Gerard Lachance."

"You seem to be fond of horses, and they seem very calm around you."

"Yes, they know me now. I stop after school and I often brush them and talk with them. They know my voice and they come to see me when I am here."

Monsieur Renaud seemed amused. He smiled when he said, "How would you like a job after school every day, feeding and brushing them?"

"Me? A real job? That pays . . . money?" I was suddenly breathless and I seemed not able to breathe. I realized I was holding my breath, and I wondered if I had heard correctly.

"Yes, of course, real money. I don't expect anyone to work for me for nothing."

"Oh, I can't believe it. Money to do something I like to do, and to be able to bring the money home to Maman." I dropped my voice in embarrassment as I realized I had spoken my thoughts out loud.

Monsieur Renaud continued questioning. "What do you think would be a fair price for your services for brushing and feeding the horses?" Monsieur Renaud's eyes twinkled as he spoke, though his voice was firm and business like.

I felt at a loss. I wanted to bring money home to Maman to help with the food and expenses. But I didn't know how much to ask for. I wanted to ask for $2.00 per week, but I didn't want the offer to be withdrawn because I asked for too much. What shall I say, I thought. Then I thought I would ask him what the job would pay and be honest with him. "Well, sir, I have no idea what a job like this would pay, but I would be so happy to be able to help out at home, and I hope you know that I would do my best, sir."

"Yes, Gerard, I can see that. I will give you $3.50 a week for five days a week. How long do you imagine it would take you to do this job?"

"Perhaps two or three hours. Well, I have never fed and watered them, though I have given them a little hay and water when they seemed to need it. They do eat oats as well, don't they?"

"Yes, they do, but they do not need to be brushed every day.

RITA J. BERON

Use your own good judgment on how often they should be brushed."

"Does any one else come to take care of them?"

"I did have a young man for a time, but he was not dependable, and I have a man who comes over the week end to see if there is enough hay and oats, but I have a feeling you will be here every day. If by chance, you could not come, I would expect you to let me know if there is any emergency. Here is my card. I live only a few doors from here, in the brownstone with the blue shutters. Now I heard you speaking to Figarro when I came this afternoon. Have you met the other two? This young filly is Carmen, and the black beauty is Don Jose."

I was surprised, and I blurted out, "You must love Bizet's music too! The opera, Carmen, was my maman's favorite, and she taught us all of the words to the most famous arias."

"You must be an unusual family. Yes, indeed, a very unusual family. You see, I used to be an opera singer in my youth, and I too appreciate Bizet's work." Monsieur Renaud looked at me and asked, "Is your mother in the music business?"

I looked at him in awe. His wavy hair was starting to be gray at his temples, but his eyes sparkled with interest, and he stood so straight and tall. "She was a pianist when she was young, and now she teaches piano lessons. And sir, I never met an opera singer up close before, but I am very happy to meet you, and I am so happy to be able to take care of your horses. Thank you, thank you! Now I must go home to my mam, because she will wonder what has kept me, and I don't want her to worry, and I have to tell her the good news, and sir . . . when would you like me to start?"

"Why tomorrow after school. But before I go, I would like to show you where you can find the oats and the hose to fill the troughs with water. If you keep them filled every day; that should be sufficient. And I would like you to stop every week on Friday afternoon for your wages." When he left, he smiled at me and shook my hand. He said, "A gentleman's agreement, does that suit you?"

FAMILY VOICES

I ran all of the way home. I ran up the steps and stumbled in the front hall door and ran to hug my mother. "Maman, you can't believe what has happened. Remember I have told you about Monsieur Renaud's horses and how I love to talk to them and pet them after school?"

"Yes, I remember. What has happened?"

"Well, I met him this afternoon, and he offered me a job. A real job, that pays $3.50 a week! I have to work every night after school for a few hours, feeding them, brushing them and seeing that they have water. And maman, I know those horses now. They are not afraid of me and they always come when I call. Their names are Figarro, Carmen and Don Jose. I will be able to bring money home to you, maman, think what that means! We will have more money for milk for Cecile! It seems like a miracle to be able to do work I like with the horses."

"It does seem to be a miracle, Gerry. I think you are one lucky young man, and I am a very fortunate mother to have you." Mam's eyes sparkled with joy and I couldn't help noticing.

I thought often that there were not too many things in our life now that made her smile. I know she still missed my papa. I have watched her change. I don't have the words to tell you how she has changed. It is like all of the joys that she kept inside waiting to bubble over are all gone and there are no bubbles left in her. She seems to go through the day without feeling much, or maybe she tries to hide her empty feelings from us. Though having Gilberte home again seems to bring joy to her. Every time she walks past mam, Gilberte stops and hugs her. She is the same with the little ones. I see tears in her eyes all day long. Gilberte says again and again that she is so happy to be home, and we all know by looking at her that her life must have been hard, even compared to ours.

When we ask her about the orphanage, she doesn't say much. I think she does not want to complain. But Maman was told by Sister Marie Therese that Gilberte was a god-send to them because of her many talents. She said Gilberte was almost too willing, it was hard not to take advantage of her many talents and to forget how young she was herself and how exhausted she could be. Maman seemed angry when she spoke of it and I know she worries about her. She is adamant when she says she will not allow Gilberte to look for work until she has been home for some time and looks and feels stronger.

    I have this happy feeling inside of me when I see all of us together around the dinner table at night. We will be all right, and now I can help too. And thank you God, for bringing Gilberte home to us again.

    I was standing on a box brushing Don Jose's coat, when someone came up behind me and put his arm around my throat. "So you're the smart ass kid who took my job!" His voice sounded menacing. His arm clutched at me harder making it difficult for me to breathe.

    I struggled to get my breath and talk. "I didn't take your job! The job was offered to me because I love taking care of horses." He released his grip a bit. "And if you are the young man who had this job before, you should talk to the boss, Monsieur Renaud."

    "I don't think I want to do that. I want my job back and if you know what's good for you, you will stop working here. I wouldn't want anything bad to happen to you, kid. You better do like I say, or you will have more trouble than you can handle." His threatening sneer left a lasting impression on me.

    He let go of me with a violent push that knocked me off of the box. Don Jose went up on his hind legs with a great loud whinny, and hit the side of his stall with his hooves. He didn't act like he wanted that boy near me or him. I don't mind saying that he scared me, but the horses didn't seem to like him either. My pants were torn and my knee was scraped and bleeding, but I was all right.

    Today was Friday and I was supposed to collect my weekly pay from Monsieur Renaud. When I appeared at his door, he asked me to come in like he always does. Then he noticed my bloody knee and my pants. Before I could say anything, he called, "Marie, please come and take care of young Gerry. He has had an accident, and he shouldn't go home like this." Then he looked at me, and said, "Then you can tell me what happened."

Marie was a gentle, well rounded, white haired lady who was Monsieur Renaud's housekeeper. She had kind eyes and red cheeks like shiny apples. She always smelled like what she was cooking, which was always good. She often had cookies and milk for me when I stopped. By now, she felt like an old aunt with whom I shared family stories. She was easy to talk to and her kitchen was always warm and cozy with smells of good food coming from the oven. She cleaned and patched my knee and made me remove my pants while she sewed them up. Afterward, I was taken back to the library where Monsieur Renaud questioned me.

"You may as well tell me what happened, Gerry. I saw Kurt, the young lad who used to work with the horses in the neighborhood awhile ago, and I wondered if he would give you trouble. Did he?"

"He didn't do much to me really. I was standing on a box to give Don Jose a little brushing before I left for home because I know he likes it so much, when Kurt came up behind me and put his arm around my neck. He told me he wanted his job back and told me I should quit or he would give me trouble. I was scared, and when he let me go he gave me a push off the box and I fell on my knee. That's all it was. I'm fine. Marie took care of my knee and my pants. But I was scared. And the funny thing is that I don't think Don Jose liked him either. When Kurt pushed me off the box, Don Jose stood up on his hind legs and hit the side of his stall."

"I will give you your money for the week, and I think I will walk home with you now, Gerry. Don't worry about Kurt. I will take care of it. I don't think he will bother you again. There will always be bullies in this world and under normal circumstances, I would ask you to stand up for yourself, but he is more than twice your age and more than twice your size. It would not be a fair match."

When I brought Monsieur Renaud into our apartment, he stopped and stared at my mother. "It's you," he said. "I watched you play the overture to a concerto when you were quite young, probably about twelve years old at the time, I would think. We were in a church, and now I am not sure of the occasion. But I thought to myself that you would have a great career in music. But forgive me, I am Monsieur Renaud."

"I am pleased to meet you, Monsieur Renaud. I recognize your name. You were my favorite tenor. When I was in school and studying music, I had opportunities to see many operas. But I am surprised you would remember me from such an obscure incident in my life." My mother blushed a little at the surprise of the meeting.

"Perhaps because it was very early in my career, and I was taken with your considerable talent. And if you forgive me for saying it, you were quite a beautiful child." Before anything else was said, Monsieur Renaud made his excuses and left for home.

I thought about the meeting between my mother and Monsieur Renaud when I was in bed that evening. Many people had told me that my mother had a wonderful talent. She often played when we were in bed before she went to sleep. I always thought it relaxed her and helped her to forget about papa. It seemed remarkable to me that Monsieur Renaud would remember her. And that he thought she had been a beautiful child.

Joe Desjardins, son of Marie-Louise Pichette Robert Desjardin and her second husband. Florina Robert and Emilienne Lachance, 12 years old.

CHAPTER VI

Emilienne's Voice

"What I mean by reading is not skimming, not being able to say as the world saith, "Oh yes, I've read that!" but reading again and again, in all sorts of moods, with an increase of delight every time, till the thing read has become a part of your system and goes forth along with you to meet any new experience you may have." C. E. Montague, A Writer's Notes on His Trade

I have a reputation in my family for always having my nose in a book. I love to read. My books are my treasures and I can easily forget what is going on around me, and take myself to new and mysterious environments that are not so traumatic and demanding day after day. The fact that I have my nose in a book whenever I have a spare minute does not make me oblivious to the state of my life. I am well aware that my mother still mourns my father's absence, and that the natural spontaneity and joy that was in her personality before he left is a rare occurrence now.

I dream of food. Beautiful roasts and vegetables covered in rich sauces. One would think I was hungry all of the time. Perhaps when I am old I will be fat. Going to bed with out enough food every night has made all of us thin. Too thin. Though Gilberte is looking better since she has been home. I can't imagine what she ate at the orphanage: she seemed nothing but eyes and bones, like a thin shadow of herself. Yet in our poor home environment,

I can see the happiness in her face. She is always hugging mam, and the little ones.

Gilberte is always anxious for me to pass on the books our mother gets for me to read. Then if she reads them too, we have a discussion about it. Now we are reading some of Shakespeare. We are also reading Voltaire, but maman believes that although he is a genius he is also a rogue. Maman said she will have us read a bit of Aristotle and Plato when we are finished with the others. She said she was always interested in the simple way he discussed his ethics. When Aristotle discussed what he believed to be the best life, and his questions of virtue, and how we shall find happiness and fulfillment, she said his meanings were clear and she wondered what we would think. She said that Santayana had once said of Aristotle that he believed that every ideal has a natural basis and everything natural has an ideal development. Maman would have been an exceptional teacher. We love how she thinks.

If mam knew what our days at work were like, she would be very upset by it. Though she may know more than what we imagine she does. But we try to shield her as much as we can. I am almost thirteen and soon Laurette will be fifteen. I still look like a tall, thin weed of a girl. But Laurette is starting to show signs of a young woman's form. Yesterday, Mr. McDermott, the supervisor in Laurette's department touched her in an inappropriate way, and her immediate reaction was to slap his face. She told me she was petrified all afternoon. She was afraid she would lose her job, because she had known others who had lost their jobs for less of an infraction. I consoled her in the street car on the way home. I really believe she is too valuable to them now. She knows her work, she does not waste time and she sews quickly and very well. We will pray tonight that she will keep her job. We couldn't do without it.

Sometimes we think we will never be able to catch up on sleep even if we could sleep as much as we wanted the rest of our lives. Our days start early and we never see the sun except on Sundays, but then we have church and chores to do at home. Maman said that God will forgive us for working on Sunday.

We don't have a choice and we try to make it fun. It is good to be with the little ones. They are no longer babies and they are unspoiled and sweet, and it is surprising how much they are learning to help.

I have noticed that we are all outgrowing our clothing and we are beginning to look shabby. One thing I learned at home, is that we must never look poor, even if we are. I am not sure if that is a French trait, or a family one, but that is so ingrained in me. We never want to be the object of people's pity. We must always look our best when sitting at the dinner table to show respect to our mother and our siblings. Our table manners must be impeccable. I know that is the manner in which my maman was raised, and she is doing her best to see that we are raised in the same way.

This evening at dinner, I looked around the dinner table at everyone. Maman said the blessing and everyone at the table had downcast eyes, except for me. I often think when I look at everyone, that my father must be missing us. I still don't understand why he left, and I don't believe that maman does either. Sometimes I think that my maman is a naive woman, even though I feel she must also be a brilliant woman. She was raised in a strict home environment under the care and teachings of her governess. Her aunt and uncle were also extremely exacting in teaching her how she must behave. From there she lived in a dormitory at a strict convent finishing school, one of the best in Montreal. Afterward, she went into an early marriage. I don't know for sure, but I believe it was arranged, just from the few things she has said about it. She never knew anything of the ways of the world. Yet, she has so much knowledge to impart to us. I only wish we had more time to learn. She has said she will teach us Latin when we are finished with the books we are reading.

Our apartment is not a long way from the St. Lawrence River. When I am yearning for the sunshine and the trees, I recall my memorized view of it and bring it out of my hiding place somewhere in my head, and it can seem so real to me. It makes me feel so tranquil and at peace. Best of all are my remembrances of the colors of the trees in the fall, and the river quietly flowing to other lands. On overcast days, the river flows by in a gray green color, rather sullen and sad, like the tears of life. When the sun appears and the sky is a brilliant blue, and I look up and see the red sumac, and green pines, my heart feels great leaps of joy, making it difficult for me to breathe. And I thank God for the gifts of His natural beauty. It is during these moments, I am glad to be alive. I know things will be better for us, I feel sure of it.

Rita J. Beron

Germaine Lachance Robert in Montreal

CHAPTER VII

Germaine's Voice

"Children are remarkable for their intelligence and ardor, for their curiosity, their intolerance of shams, the clarity and ruthlessness of their vision." Aldous Huxley collected essays

Maman considers me the delicate one, but now that I am nine years old and in school, I am sure I am past the childhood disease phase. I have already had measles and mumps and chicken pox. What more can there be?

Well, I am home from school with a cold, and maman insisted I stay home, though every one else at school is sick too. Colds must be contagious because everyone is coughing. I love school, but it is kind of nice to be home because then I can be a help to my maman. My sister Simone is seven now and she is very helpful too. We feel so sad about Cecile. She was sent back home from school today. Sister Marie Jean said that Cecile is suffering from malnutrition. Her arms and legs are too thin and her stomach is too big. We are all too thin, but maman says we had a better beginning because she had milk for us from her breasts and she nursed us for two years. When Cecile was born, my maman lost her milk. And when she was a baby, cow's milk made her sick. Cow's milk doesn't make her sick now, but we seldom have enough money to buy it. But when I am working I will be able to help maman with food and milk money, so Cecile's strength and health can improve.

I just have to talk about my sister Gilberte. She started working when she was twelve years old. She started sewing leather gloves with my older sister Emilienne. The girls work for $3.00 a week. They work twelve hours a day, six days a week, though there was a law passed recently that the work-days will be shortened to eleven hours. Maman said the law did not include the small boutiques and the shops that did not employ many people and some of the designer's salons. Just the large manufacturers were affected. So my sisters will still work twelve hour days.

Probably you don't know, but most children start working for $2.50 a week. It may go to $3.00 or so. Women start making about $5.00 a week for 72 hours, though again it depends on whether they work for a large manufacturer or not. And men start at about $8.00 per week. Maman says I have a head for business. And that she expects great things from me.

Gilberte is now fifteen years old, and she found a new job that pays a bit more. But her hours are more erratic and when they are working on many designs for a show, some nights she works all hours. She is now working for a couturier designer in old town, near where we live. She can walk to work. She is so excited to be sewing beautiful clothes. Every day she comes home like a changed person and it is hard to keep her quiet. She speaks of the clients they have, and how they want their clothes to look like the designs from Paris. Gilberte is so honest. We all wondered how long she would last in that job. But the top designer seems to like my sister's ideas. Can you imagine? I wouldn't be brave enough to tell them what I thought. She asked Gilberte's opinion on the new dress Gilberte had just finished sewing. So much of the work is hand stitching. Gilbert told her she would remove the large bow on the shoulder. And when the designer looked up and asked why, my sister responded that any dress should enhance the figure of the woman it was designed for, and simplicity was best for a small petite person. Simply put, the bow was overpowering. We all clapped when Berte said the designer removed the bow, stepped back, carefully looked at it, and said she agreed. She told Berte that she had a natural fashion sense and was happy to have her ideas. Though Berte is smart enough to know that the designer would never admit that someone else has a good idea in front of the other workers. All of the best ideas must come from the designer. Berte just takes it in stride as part of the job. But to watch her tell of her days at work, with all of the ups and downs and the demanding clientele is like watching a play. I used to think she should be a writer. She makes it so interesting and she never leaves a thing out! Maman was clapping and enjoying the animated conversation with genuine joy. Wasn't that good? I think my mam is so proud that my sisters are growing up and becoming lovely young women. And she should take a bow for that.

 I never knew what good breeding was when I was small, but I understand now after listening to my mam. It has far more to do with manners, which means showing kindness and consideration to everyone we meet, no matter how high or how low they are on the social scale. Breeding has nothing to do with the accumulation of wealth. Mam says wealthy people may be well bred, but sometimes they are not, but so may middle class and poor people.

 And my brother Gerry is really the man in the house now. Even his voice is changing. He is almost twelve and kind of bossy, and in some ways he is a real pain, but we all know he has a big heart. He would do anything for any one of us if we needed him. And we would do anything for him, if it were possible. He is as good as God made brothers, but you understand how brothers are.

 He still takes care of Monsieur Renaud's horses and occasionally, Monsieur Renaud takes him riding on Saturday afternoons. Starting next week he will work another job for a grocer, delivering groceries on Saturdays. Maman wants him to stay in school as long as he can, so he can have a better job some day. Maman has always said, he loves the horses and many boys his age who are working full time in factories don't make any more than he does.

And I have lots of plans for myself too. One day I will marry a wonderful man who will love me as much as I love him. None of this so called arranged marriage for me. What happened to mam shouldn't have happened. She didn't deserve it. Now that I am so grown up, and I stay up later, I hear my sisters talking once in awhile. I don't really remember my father very much, but I know they loved him. And mam has always been courageous, and wonderful to us. But it is the beginning of the 20s, and the world war is over, and it is a new era.

There was even a lot of strikes last year. More than 30,000 workers were involved. Maman picked up a news bulletin at the grocery store today that was part of a report by Felix Marois. I think maman said he was Commissioner of the Quebec Trades Act. He wrote about the reasons for the strikes last year and maman asked that we all read it. And then she questioned us about it and asked us what we thought. It is like mam to make a lesson out of the information of everything she thinks we should be aware. It made us realize once more that we have not been alone in our poverty. The workers had been asked to make sacrifices during the war for the "great effort" with a promise of an increase in wages as soon as the war was over, but now the war had been over for some time and nothing had changed. And now the cost of living had been made out of reach for them, which was unjust. They thought the rich had grown richer, and they said that this was fine, as long as it was not at the expense of the whole nation. We talked about this for a long time, and mam asked us once more what we thought should be done. It was fun to be treated like a thinking older person. It seemed that the workers who had struck could not afford food or clothing for their families, and they saw no help coming. We all cried a little when we read this and talked about it. Felix Marois' words touched our souls. It was too real a reminder of our own lives. But we have a mother who is educated and she made it better somehow by her teaching and her encouragement. She is able to explain what happens in a way that we can easily understand. She told us that in Montreal, particularly, the working class paid the price of industrial growth without receiving anything in the way of benefits in all of the years that she had been a student interested in politics and the labour movement. And she did not think it would change any time soon. She said there should be more women in politics. And I told her I agreed with her. More women indeed!

Maman smiled at me. It seems I make her smile a lot.

Gilberte Lachance Beron and Simone Lachance

CHAPTER VIII

SIMONE'S VOICE

"Without sacrifice there is no resurrection. Nothing grows and blooms save by giving. All you try to save in yourself wastes and perishes." Andre Gide, The Fruits of the Earth

When I have been in school with the nuns, I think about the life they have, and I sometimes wish I could have that life some day. They have an education and they teach children and they have time to think and pray. And they can help people, poor people like us. But when I look at maman and Cecile and all of us when we are seated around the dinner table at night, the rare times when we are all together like on Sundays, I think my job will be to look after my maman.

Cecile may never have good health. My heart cries when I look at her. She needs me and maman to look after her. Some day I will have a job too and I will be able to help.

Maman has taught me to crochet and knit and I can do beautiful sweaters. But I need more practice in sewing. Until now I have sewed only simple things. I haven't tried to sew a complicated dress yet. But maman said that my embroidery work is very beautiful. She has a way of appreciating all that we do, and all that we try to do.

My brother Gerry has always been very good to me. When he gets home from taking care of the horses, he often reads to me and then I read to him. My reading is doing better now. It is my second year in school and I do love it. The schools are crowded and I share a desk with another girl, and we share a book too. I don't have books to bring home. So Gerry helps me with my reading in the evenings before I go to bed. I hold Cecile and we all read together, though Cecile is not reading quite yet. She loves the stories and the pictures in the books. And I have noticed lately that she is eating better than she has before, and is not as pale. She really is quite beautiful, and maman says she has my father's eyes and mouth. Perhaps she will be strong enough to go back to school soon.

Yesterday, a boy knocked at our door and he said he was Gerry's friend. He spoke with some kind of an accent. He introduced himself as Pavel Yelitch. He seemed to know enough French to make himself understood. He asked if my mother was at home. Well, after we spoke to him for awhile, we realized that his mother was in labor and they had no money for a doctor, and Gerry had told him our maman delivered babies. So maman took me aside and asked me if I felt up to helping her. I was a bit afraid and I felt frightened because I had never seen a baby born before and because the boy was so dirty and thin. But I felt good that maman would trust me with such a thing. Maman gave me a basket with clean towels and freshly laundered sheets and soap, and she took a bag with sterilized cloths to wrap the baby in. Dr. Bujold had given her the few instruments including forceps that he used in the delivery of babies just before he died, and a book of the types of deliveries. Maman kept the instruments sterilized and ready in case of emergencies. She was able to leave Cecile with our neighbor, Catherine Donovan. The last thing maman did before we left, was write a note to the children to let them know where we had gone.

Pavel showed us the way to his house down by the river in an industrial area with very poor housing. We had never been down there before, but maman had remarked once when we were out for a walk during the summer, that people lived there to be close to their work. When we stepped into the house, I could hear my maman hold her breath. It was surprising to me that she could remain calm. The floors were dirt and there did not appear to be any inside plumbing. The rooms were dark with gas lamps, and the air was damp and fetid. The room was too hot where the stove was and too damp and chilly in the other rooms. There were four young children, barefoot, dirty, and too thin, in the main room. Pavel's mother was in the back room lying on a hard bed, perspiring and in pain. My maman asked Pavel if they had a water supply in the house. He took her to a closet and showed her a pump. She told him to boil some water. Then she examined his mother, who was in the last stages of labor. Maman said she was fully dilated and the baby was in the birth canal. Madame Yelitch's eyes looked like she was frightened. Maman quickly spread clean towels under Pavel's mother, and I ran to get him to be the interpreter for her, so she would know what my mother was doing and she would not be afraid. Maman spoke in a soft voice, and Pavel translated, telling her when to bear down and push and when to breathe. Maman said the baby was in some kind of a posterior presentation and it would be more difficult for the baby with its chin pressed down to get around the curve in the birth canal, but maman helped the baby to rotate naturally and it was born all right. I think I held my breath through the whole thing. It was a tiny little baby and it was a girl. She started crying and mam wrapped her in the sterile cloth and placed her in her maman's arms while my maman did something to Madame Yelitch's stomach to help remove the last of the afterbirth. By that time the water was finally boiling and maman gave Madame Yelitch a gentle washing. She looked so relieved and happy. By the looks of all of them, and where they lived, I knew they really did not have a way to wash very often, or very much to eat. I am not even sure where they could wash their clothes or go to the bathroom. The beds were not much more than boards on the dirt floors. But I think the worst part of all was that they had no windows and it was hard to breathe in there because it smelled so bad. Before we left, maman had a talk with Pavel. She asked him if there was any food in the house to give his mother. Maman also asked him something strange, at least I thought it was unlike her to ask such a thing. She asked him if he knew what his father paid for the rent. He told her twelve dollars a month. He said his family stayed in this place because they could not afford bus fare. My maman looked angry and told him that the average rent in Montreal was eight dollars and seventy five cents, and even where she lived it was five dollars per month. Maman asked who the landlord was. When he told her, maman had a determined look on her face. I knew she was planning something. She also said she would find out if there were any vacancies in our building. And it would still be within walking distance of work. Then she told Pavel what he must do for his mother to keep her and the baby clean. And that she must have food to be able to produce milk for her new baby.

When we were walking home, maman said now she was aware of why the childbirth statistics in this part of Montreal were so bad. "The problems that exist here, my sweet girl, are that people live under such crowded and sub-standard conditions and the fact that we still don't have purified water in areas like this, or any dairies that have pasteurized milk, all play a part in those statistics. As you saw today, there is a reason why even back in 1915, 42% of the forty five thousand children under two years of age died of some kind of infantile diarrhea. I remember those statistics so well. So many people we knew lost babies that year. And even today, in this part of Montreal the mortality rate is still more than 33%. I guess we should consider it something of a miracle that we still have our Cecile."

"Oh, maman, I hope God forgives me for feeling poor. After today I will remember the Yelitch family and how they have been forced to live. Didn't you tell me once that many people come here looking for a job and a better life? Well, I know we are poor. There is never enough food or money for clothing. But I think we are rich because we have you. And you have never let us down.

"Thank you, Simone. You are a sweet girl with a kind heart. What do you think we should do about the Yelitch family?"

"I think we should find out if there is an apartment available in our building, and let them know about it. I know that everyone in our building has a hard time. No one has enough money to live, but it seems to me that everyone here has a heart, and maybe between all of us we can do something to help them."

"I can tell you belong to my family, my girl." My maman hugged me, and continued. "I wanted to ask you what you thought. I feel the same way, but we must ask everyone what they can spare in our building. I will start sewing some baby clothes and I will crochet a baby bonnet and sweater and the important things a baby needs. If they moved to our building, things would be easier and they would have more money for food and a more healthful place to live. You and I will make a plea to the rest of our family and see what they will say."

"Oh, maman, you know what they will say."

"Yes, I do know. I don't think they will hesitate for a minute, and I know they will share what they have. And their hearts will give and give again for the Yelitch family.

Maman found out that there was a three bedroom apartment in our building that was just vacated that was a bit larger than ours, and it was $5.50 per month. So we asked Gerry to bring Pavel home one night after school to see it. He was so happy to see the bedrooms with windows, and the kitchen with a stove to cook on, and a bathroom with a water heater for when the family needed baths, and every where there were clean wooden floors. He had tears in his eyes when he ran home. They moved into the apartment when Mr. Yelitch was off of work on Sunday. They had very little furniture to move.

My maman went to the St. Vincent de Paul Society and asked for help for the Yelitch family. Pavel went along with his mother so he could translate for her. St. Vincent de Paul had been kind to us once when we were desperate for rent money. Maman had found out that there was a lot of paper work to be filled out, and then they would help you get what you needed. Though it was not meant to be an ongoing charity, but to help when families were in desperate need. The Yelitch family was able to get beds and some simple furniture that were clean and still had some wear in them. They were also given some clean clothes and some used pots and pans and dishes. All of the people in our building also contributed something, whether it was potatoes, or tinned vegetables or fresh ones. The two butchers who lived in our building contributed some stew meat and some milk. The Yelitch family now lived on the floor beneath us, and they greeted my maman like she was some kind of saint. I don't know what a real saint is. But they looked at her with wonder in their faces and eyes filled with admiration and gratitude. But I believe as my maman believes, that we should always do everything possible to help people who need it.

Cecile Lachance dressed for a costume party

CHAPTER IX

CECILE'S VOICE

"Then I want to sit and listen and have someone talk, tell me things—their life histories—books they have read, things they have done—new worlds! Not to say anything—to listen and listen and be taught."
  Anne Morrow Lindbergh—Bring Me a Unicorn

I am the one who always sits and listens and watches the scene around me. Most people don't believe I have a voice of my own or they believe I can't speak, because I choose to be quiet. For a long, long time, I did not have energy to talk and it was easier to listen. And then I discovered that I learned so much when I was quiet and observing. It was like reading a book. My maman holds me and cuddles me often. I sometimes think she is willing me to be strong, by her love and her encouragement. And I do feel stronger and I have been eating more. The first day I went to school, I shared a desk with three other five year olds. There weren't any books for us and I couldn't follow what the teacher was telling us to do, though I knew she was trying to teach us the alphabet by demonstrating the letters on the blackboard. There was a lot of noise and children coughing. The nun was kind but she said she felt I should be at home. She wrote a note for my maman saying that I was suffering from malnutrition and when I was stronger, she could send me again. I asked my maman what malnutrition was and she explained it to me. Then she told me we were blest because I had lived in spite of all of our problems and a lack of milk and enough food.

While I have been home, my brother Gerry and my sister Simone have been teaching me, and I am learning! And my maman makes it easy to learn. I love to listen to them read to me. I look at the words. They are like little pictures of meaning and I am beginning to recognize them and I can figure out the words.

My brother Gerry makes us all laugh. Emilienne says that he is a natural comedian. When we have problems, he does not let us feel sad for long. Soon he has us laughing because of something he said, or just the way he said it. He can mimic anyone, and even though maman says it isn't always kind to mimic, she understands that we all need to laugh.

My sisters Gilberte, Emilienne, and Laurette all went to a party last Sunday afternoon. It was so exciting to watch them getting dressed. A grown up party just doesn't happen. They all wore dresses they had made from cloth scraps that the designer gave Gilberte. She was able to design dresses for all of the girls in a way that used up all of the large and smaller pieces of cloth. The designer knows that Gilberte loves her job and knew she needed clothes and she was trying to be helpful. Who else would work that hard for so little? One of the girls at the party brought her cousin from the United States. His name was Raymond Beron and I think he liked Gilberte and he thought she was older. She had a shy smile on her face as she talked about him. She told him she was too young to date and her mother would not allow it. Berte said he looked so surprised when she told him she was fifteen. She said he told her she was a nice girl. He spoke only English, and Gilberte thought "nice" meant "pretty" in English. She replied, in her limited English, "Me not nice, but me good." My older sisters work with English speaking supervisors, so they have learned English in the last five years and they all laughed at what Berte had said, and I could tell she felt humiliated. Maman said her French is so perfect, that she knew when Berte had the opportunity to learn English, her English would be perfect too.

I see all of my sisters turning into very attractive young ladies. I wonder if I will be attractive when I am older. Maman sometimes gets a faraway look in her eyes when she looks at me. She tells me it is a pity that my father never saw me, because I look so much like him. And Gerry tells me I have his eyes, his mouth and I even have his walk, which I am told is very distinctive. Maman said distinctive means very special. And when I ask if she thinks I will be attractive too, she says not to worry, I will be a beauty. I really don't care about that, but I do want to learn. I want to be healthy so I feel like running out in the sunshine.

When the girls sit around and visit during dinner, I am sometimes allowed to stay up just to be with them. I love to listen to them, because their worlds are so filled with life. I understand that they have a hard life, but they don't show that side to me. They laugh and their discussions are full of humor about what they have observed and learned.

I don't know if my family knows how much I think and watch and notice. Because I am quiet, they don't realize that I understand everything. You see, I know I am getting stronger, and soon I will be able to run and play in the park. And when I grow up, I will help my family by working and we will all sit around the dinner table eating and laughing together.

Diana Lachance at the piano—about 1950

CHAPTER X

DIANA'S VOICE

"Action is consolatory. It is the enemy of thought and the friend of flattering illusions. Only in the conduct of our action can we find the sense of mastery over the Fates." Joseph Conrad, *Nostromo*

It is often frustrating for me to come to the realization that I can only do so much to make any substantial changes in our lives. After watching Cecile's health slowly improve and her strength increase, I decided to take her back to school to see if the crowded conditions had improved in any way. We arrived early so I would have the opportunity to speak with the teacher.

Sister Marie Jean took me to the front of the room where her desk was and she invited me to sit down. The children were coming into the room. I could see that there were still three little girls at a desk, and I asked Sister if there was any hope for an improvement in the class size and the book supplies that were used in the class. She said that in the eastern section of Montreal, the schools were all inadequate for the thousands of students, and the money allotted to the Public Catholic schools was inadequate for the amount of students. I asked her how that could be, since all Public Protestant, and Public Catholic schools should be allotted an equal amount per student. She said that she did not know who exactly made the rules. Though she thought the Bishop or the Archbishop of the diocese would know.

I brought Cecile home with me. I didn't believe her strength was equal to the strain of trying to learn in an environment like that. Perhaps one day, but not now. I am determined to learn why Public Catholic Schools are inadequately funded, and I will teach her at home.

It was two days afterwards that I left Cecile with my neighbor, Catherine Donovan, while I took the street car to the diocesan offices of the Bishop and the Archbishop. I had been told when I telephoned that one of them would see me for a short time. I prayed that I would have the right words. I kept asking myself, "Who am I that I feel I can go to them?" My mind answered, "I am a mother who is interested in the education her children are receiving," And I would see what could be done.

I was seated in a waiting room outside the offices. When I inquired at the desk, the young man answered that they were aware of my visit, and that it would be a few minutes before I could see the Archbishop.

I noticed by the clock on the desk that I had waited twenty minutes and I wondered if he had forgotten that I was still there waiting. He had been intently reading at his desk. He looked up as I approached. "Oh, yes, I see you are still here."

"May I see the Archbishop now?"

"I will see if he can see you."

Within a few minutes, the Archbishop came out to meet me, and after the proper introductions were made, he invited me into his office.

"Thank you for seeing me, your excellency. I know you are a busy man."

He asked me to be seated, and asked, "How may I help you, Madame Lachance?"

"It has recently come to my attention that the division of funds for the two public systems, the Catholic Public Schools and the Protestant Public Schools are divided unequally. I always understood that the taxes that were collected were to be divided equally for each student regardless of the school. That would be the only just and equitable way."

"You are right, Madame Lachance, that is the way it was

intended, but it has always been that the funds are divided more or less equally, but actually the Protestant Public Schools get about ten thousand more."

"But I don't understand that. They have less than 25% of the student population and they receive more than the Public Catholic Schools who have more than 75% of the student populations? Why aren't we doing something about that?"

"My dear young woman, I regularly attend these meetings and it would do me no good to complain. The system has been in place now for many years. They argue that the subsidized Catholic Schools that receive tuition make up the difference. Of course, none of the Catholic schools that are private and charge tuition share what they get. They get no other help from the taxes, and the tuition is very little, so in fact, that reasoning is not correct."

"I don't understand how you can go to these meetings and witness the unjust situation and not try to correct it. I am sorry your excellency, I can't understand. I was taught at my school that we should all try to make the lives of the poor better by helping in any way that we can. I have a large family and since my husband left, it has been a constant struggle. Not only has it been impossible for me to keep them fed and clothed adequately, but the schools, with the crowded conditions and no books or other necessities make learning next to impossible. The Catholic Public Schools have no money for maintenance or heat, and the nuns have to work so hard to make it possible for the children to learn. Most working class people in Montreal live in substandard housing, and really are not able to feed or clothe their families adequately. Most of the people in my building see themselves as unable to educate their children. Because the adults are so poorly paid, children are forced to work at such an early age. It is just not an equitable situation. And while I think of it, I have been in church on Sundays with my family, and we have often heard the priests tell the working people not to strike. Their families are starving and they have no money for clothing for their families, and they are to do nothing? The priest said that there was holiness in acceptance. I was appalled at what he said. Most of the people listen to what their priests say. They look up to them as being educated and fair, when so often they have no one to turn to, or in some cases, no one who even speaks their language.

The Archbishop looked down and shook his head. "We are told again and again that we should not get involved in politics, and politics are exactly what this is all about. You may not be aware, young woman, but all of this just reflects the great political and economic power of the Anglo-protestant minority."

"You are an educated man, a man of great authority. I beg of you, try to change the system. Stand up for your people. Do what you can to help them. And politics be damned. Show the people on the Anglo side that you will stand up and speak for your people. At this time in our history, we have many social ills that need to be addressed. We need hospitals and medical care that the poor working man can afford. We have very little on the east side of the city, really nothing that the impoverished working class can count on. Our water is still polluted in some areas of the city, our dairies are still producing non pasteurized milk, and our infant mortality rate has only improved in these last years to 33%. I have noticed when any improvements occur, it is for the West Side of Montreal."

The Archbishop looked flustered, but he looked up at me for the first time. I had risen from my chair when I was speaking without realizing it, and was feeling disconcerted and embarrassed now. He said, "You are an educated and articulate young woman, and I can see that you feel deeply about the fate of your family and the people you've seen suffering. Tell me, where were you educated?"

"I graduated from the Convent of St. Laurent. The Sisters of Sainte-Croix were our teachers, and they were wonderful women. They cared about people and they showed it in the way they taught us."

"That convent is one of a kind. Very exclusive, but excellent. You must have come from a family of means."

"I was raised by a wealthy uncle. In fact, I grew up in a

mansion, much like the one you live in. But not all of my family were wealthy. I just happen to think that if God has bestowed his gifts on us, whether it is mental ability, or education or both, it is our duty to help our fellow man when it is possible. And I do think you could do endlessly wonderful things for our people." For the first time, I paused . . . "And perhaps I should leave. If I have offended you, I am deeply sorry. I did not intend to do that or to speak that way when I came to see you. But if I had to do it over again, I would probably do the same. Thank you for seeing me, your excellency. Now I must hurry home to cook what I can for my hungry children."

The Archbishop removed his glasses and took out his handkerchief to wipe his face as he stepped out of his office to speak to his young assistant. "That was quite a young woman, yes quite a young woman. See what you can find out about Madame Gaudiose Lachance. I believe she gave you her address. For the first time in years, I want to ignore the policy we have had about not getting involved in politics. I believe we have been wrong."

It was a few days after my visit to the Archbishop's office, that the young man who had been sitting at the desk, knocked at my door. I was shocked to see him, and my immediate reaction was surprise and embarrassment. I wondered if my words with the Archbishop had gone too far. "Are you here to collect a written apology from me?"

He stammered and then he smiled, "Why no. Not at all. I am here at the Archbishop's request to inquire if you could come to his office one afternoon to help him draft a document that states all of the social and economic ills that need improving in Montreal. And he said if you have children at home, bring them along. I don't know what you said to him, but he shook his head and said not getting involved in politics was wrong. He also thought you were quite an articulate young woman."

"I can't believe it. I was taught to have respect for my elders, and respect for our church leaders, but something made me speak like I did. Since my husband left, I had no way to support myself and my children, and I have seen many things I didn't know existed. My children have had to work, so I am familiar with a lack of laws that cover child labor practices. I am a midwife when there is a need and people need my help, and I teach music lessons and my children at home. I have tried to do my best, but . . ." I started to cry, and I don't know why. I guess I had been nervous about what I had said ever since I had seen the Archbishop. I took out my handkerchief and dabbed at my eyes. "Please forgive me, I didn't know what to expect when I saw you."

"Will you be able to come? I need to give the Archbishop an answer."

"I could come, but it may be easier for him to come here. I have a little one that is still not in school, and I have three others that come after school. The three older girls don't get home until late."

"Oh, I see. I will tell him. What day would be best?"

I thought for a second, and wondered about food. "Tomorrow is fine, but I must warn him. I won't have enough food to offer him even a simple dinner. I am sorry about that. Except for that, he could stay longer and we could work till later. Oh, and tell him I would appreciate having any newspapers he may have that he has already read. I pick up news bulletins when I can in the grocery store, but I don't have money for a newspaper."

Cecile was looking at me and I am sure she was wondering why I had become so honest with a stranger about our lack of food. Perhaps later I would explain to her that the Archbishop looked very well fed, and we had scant food in the house that we would have to stretch for ourselves. Not even enough for one full meal for all of us but it would have to do. It would be a few days before we could get groceries. The girls were paid every two weeks now, and Gerry was still paid on Fridays. The food we had would not do for the Archbishop. But I do have some flour, some sugar and two eggs left, so perhaps I could make a cake, I thought. No, no I can't do that. I will need that to make pancakes or something for the children.

I decided to forget about the lack of food. If he came

promptly by 2:00 p.m. we could work till I needed to make dinner. And we could accomplish everything he wants to know. I picked up Cecile and expained to her who was coming. She was quiet like she always is, but she seemed to be excited about the possibility of seeing an Archbishop up close. I spoke my thoughts to Cecile while I rocked her. I had always told her everything when I held her. She never really answered but she seemed to like the sound of my voice. I told her, perhaps, it would be good for the Archbishop to see what living is like in a poor family. Sometimes by living in a religious community one can become isolated, unless you are the kind of priest or nun who works in social services out among the people. She listened and then she surprised me. She said quite a lot and in perfect French.

"I think it will be very good for him to come maman. I know he will be surprised and pleased to be with us. Maybe he was a poor boy when he was very young, but has forgotten what it was like. I want to meet him. I will ask him to pray for me so I can be healthy. You see, maman, I want to run out in the sunshine."

"Oh, my darling girl." I squeezed back my need to cry and I cuddled my youngest daughter. God listened to prayers.

The next afternoon promptly at 2:00p.m, as we watched out of our second floor window, we saw a large black chauffeur driven automobile stop at the corner. We knew it must be the Archbishop. Cecile seemed so interested. She watched out of the window till he entered our building. Then she ran to the door and waited.

We opened the door just as he and his chauffeur were about to knock "Welcome to our home, your excellency."

"Thank you for inviting us to your home. We don't have opportunities like this to visit people in the diocese."

"You are welcome. Please come in." Then I noticed that the chauffeur was carrying a huge basket. And it smelled like food.

"I hope you don't mind. We brought food enough for dinner for you and your family so we might have the pleasure of meeting all of them and having dinner with you."

FAMILY VOICES

"Thank you. That is very generous. Yes, . . . that is very kind of you and I . . ."

"Please, don't thank me. You were very gracious to offer your assistance. You see, I need your vision and your interest. You see all of this from a personal perspective, because you have gone through it, and it is you who are helping me."

We sat at the dining room table and the Archbishop spread out some notebooks, and some books on current government policies. Cecile had been watching everyone very quietly. But she came forward and I introduced her to the Archbishop. I could tell by his look that he was aware that she was suffering from malnutrition. Some of the telltale signs were still apparent. She walked up to him and looked into his face. "You are a holy person, aren't you? Could I sit in your lap?"

"Why, I would like that."

He picked her up and she looked at him and said, "I need your help. I would like you to pray for me. I want to be strong so I can run out and see the sun and the trees."

The archbishop looked thoughtful. "I would be happy to pray for you. Soon you will be stronger." He looked at me as if for an explanation.

I am sure his young assistant had told him everything I had said to him when he came to see me, so I wasn't exactly sure what he wanted explained when, Cecile, my daughter who rarely speaks, began to tell her story in a slow and thoughtful way. "Sister told my maman I am suffering from malnutrition. You see, my papa left my maman about five months before I was born, and my maman lost her milk because she was not well herself. She said I am her miracle because I am still living, even though we didn't have enough food or milk. So I know that God wants me to live, but I am hoping you will remind Jesus that I need to be stronger, that is if you think He has the time to help me. I know there are many people all over the world that need His help." She looked up at his face and said. "Now I will sit and watch and will not bother you. But thank you." Cecile turned on her knees and kissed his cheek, and went to sit in a small rocking chair by the dining room table.

He looked emotional as he touched his cheek . . ."You are a very surprising and wonderful child. I promise you I will keep you in my prayers every day." He looked teary eyed as he spoke to her, then suddenly he cleared his throat and picked up some of the notebooks he had brought. The archbishop looked at me and said, "I suppose we should start. We have a lot of things to consider."

"I have been thinking of everything I spoke to you about when I was at your office, and I realized afterward that we really did not have any time for discussion. I just spoke of everything that concerned me and left. That really wasn't fair of me. It is just that there are so many social inequities that should be taken care of. If you would like me to stop now and again, and if I talk too fast, let me know. I am far from being an expert on anything. It is just that my life has made me doubly aware of the situations that exist for the people who live in poverty. And I know from struggling to survive myself that many have it much more difficult than I."

"You mentioned a few days ago in my office that there was a lack of adequate housing for the poor working classes. What do you know about that?"

"So much of the housing is substandard, particularly in this area. Damp, airless, dark rooms are common. They often have dirt floors, no inside plumbing of any kind, a small inadequate stove, no windows. Diseases are prevalent among the people who live there, and infant mortality is still so high." His excellency was writing fast, and his chauffeur seemed to be taking some kind of shorthand. When they could not keep up, they would raise their hand to stop me, or ask a question for me to clarify something specific. Then I went on. "Montreal is still so dependent for so much of its public health assistance on the work of private voluntary agencies. Of course, I have never been a patient in a hospital, but I have observed that a few hospitals do have departments that take care of public health assistance. I have also noticed that when there are institutions that develop an interest in public health services, instead of adopting metropolitan-wide services, the tendency has been to expand their individual spheres of activity without much regard for the gaps and lack of coordination in other parts of the city." I let them have the time to write that down, then I continued. "The problem is that the large heavily populated sections of the city are left without any access to public health services, and there is a real scarcity of medical facilities in the heavily populated areas of the east-end. When there is an acute need, there is no help available. I know because I have delivered babies in apartments where no one should have to live, not animals, and surely not human beings. No one else was available, and in most cases, they do not have the money. Tuberculosis and Diphtheria are still a health menace here in Montreal. In fact, we lost a daughter at the age of four years old, with Diphtheria. Perhaps because Montreal did not develop a systematic program to control it. In so many cases through all of the years, everything to improve the situation has been discretionary and of unequal distribution. When it was understood what the causes were, something should have been done about it. I believe that now in 1921, most of Montreal has pure water, but there are still areas that do not, and we don't have pasteurized milk in many areas.

The Archbishop looked up, took out his handkerchief and wiped his forehead. "You know that there are some French Canadians who have money and own homes."

"Yes, of course I know that. But as a segment of the French population, there are not great numbers of them, and I know that there is a growing middle class. But there is still a class of people who have never had a chance to accomplish anything. And it is not because they are lazy, or stupid. They work 11 and 12 hour days for little money and there is also much unemployment. They are unable to feed and clothe their families and they have had no help. It is because of the social inequities that exist. The unfair wage practices of the large manufacturers and owners of factories who hire people and pay them as little as they can, are one example. They have thought only of their own gain, without consideration for the worker's needs."

We had a discussion for quite some time when I could hear Simone and Germaine come through the entrance and hang up their clothes.

"Is the Archbishop here, maman?" Simone's eyes were large with excitement and Germaine came into the room and walked over to the Archbishop, "I am so honored to meet you your Excellency. My name is Germaine and this is my sister Simone. Our brother Gerry will be home soon too, but he is taking care of the horses. He does that every day after school before he comes home. He has a real job and he loves being able to help out at home."

His excellency, the Archbishop looked astonished, but answered calmly, "Why I am honored to meet you, Germaine, and you Simone. Your mother and I are becoming acquainted and discussing the social inequities that exist in our city."

"Yes, I know. We discussed it last night at dinner. Maman always uses a discussion in politics, or a news bulletin as a tool to give us a lesson in social studies. We love it. She is a good teacher."

"Yes, you are lucky to have her for your mother." Then he looked at me and asked, "Madame Lachance, do you need to stop for dinner or a snack for the children? Our work should not interfere with your usual routine."

"When it is available, I want them to have a snack or something, because they always want to wait for their older sisters who come home around 8:00 p.m. They leave at six in the morning, but they don't return till 8:00. They still work twelve-hour days. The businesses they are in were not covered by the Industrial Establishment Act. There are few inspectors who ever enter those establishments . . . Forgive me, I feel like I have been wound up and can't stop talking . . . I would be very happy to make us a cup of tea and I know you brought a large basket of food, but I didn't check what you brought. Would you care for any food?"

FAMILY VOICES

"No thank you. I usually eat my dinner around 8:00pm. So that will be fine for me, but I would enjoy a cup of tea with you and the children. Perhaps, with your permission, they could have milk and cookies. And the milk is pasteurized."

I guess I don't have to mention all of the details of the visit. In a sense, it was wonderful for me and the children. We all felt that by talking to him and telling him of our concerns for poor people, we brought a sense of reality back into his life. And we felt there was hope for better working conditions, and medical facilities and housing. He asked the older girls what they would change about their work if they could. They all said they would like an hour off for their lunch, so they would have time to be out in the sunshine in a park. He was a first hand witness to my young children, how thin they all were, and the long hours of work that was their daily routine, and I believe it opened his eyes. Especially when he was told they had already been working for six years. Gilberte had been working for five years, but even though she refuses to talk about it, I know her year at the orphanage was more difficult than anything we could imagine. I was proud of my children's reactions with his excellency. They all asked him pertinent questions, and they seemed to enjoy him, and I know from watching his face, he loved every minute of it. I wondered if he had come from a large family himself. He seemed so at home with them and all of their conversation. He discussed the school situation with them, how many students there were to one teacher, and their needs for books and heat when the weather was cold.

The food the Archbishop brought was more than enough for a wonderful dinner for all of us. He brought a whole baked ham, au gratin potatoes, fresh green beans, salads, fruits, 4 liters of milk, a tin of tea, two cakes and cookies. We learned that his sister's son was the young man who was acting as his Chauffeur and Secretary. We put the extra leaves in the table so that it would accommodate all ten of us. There was laughter, and even a few tears, but my children will remember this evening always.

I was made to realize how fast my children were becoming

adults when my son Gerry came into the kitchen after his work was finished this evening. "Mam, do you think you could teach me to dance?"

He took me by surprise, "Why, Gerry, I didn't know you had an interest in dancing."

"One of my friends from school is going to have a dance at his house when we have our summer vacation. He said all his sisters can dance. His uncle gave them a Victrola that plays records. Can you imagine that, mam? I think it sounds like it would be fun."

"I think it sounds like fun too. I married right out of school, so my dances were few, but through my music department at school, we did have some dance lessons. I believe I can show you the basics."

"What will we do for music, mam?"

"Why, we will have to sing! And there is some room to dance in the kitchen and around the dining room table. We'll manage."

Soon Germaine and Simone were dancing too. Gerry would pick up Cecile and they would dance while he sang and twirled and twirled. Cecile would laugh till tears streamed down her cheeks. It made me happy to see them laugh.

My older girls are growing up. I am sure that it will not be long till Laurette is married. She speaks of a young man from work that she seems to care for who has treated her with respect and kindness. And Gilberte has been writing to Raymond Beron from Duluth, Minnesota. They have exchanged pictures. He sent her money so she would have her picture taken for him. I believe he is nine years older than she is. If he has hopes of marrying her, he will have to wait till she grows up. Though the way the years are flying, the day will come sooner than I think. Mimi has also said that she has met an artist, a handsome man who has taste and intelligence. So you see, in the next few years I see myself losing a part of my beloved family. Though, I know they must have a life, just as I have had mine. I do hope they wait long enough to really know the men they will marry. I know that one does not truly know a man till one is married. And I suppose the same can be said of a woman.

FAMILY VOICES

THE FINAL CHAPTER

"One always dies too soon—or too late. And yet one's whole life is complete at that moment, with a line drawn neatly under it, ready for the summing up."
Jean-Paul Sartre

She passed in and out of consciousness, but when she was lucid, she could recognize the familiar faces of her family hovering near and she knew she would die here, in this room, and her soul would go before God to be judged. She believed this because she had been taught this in her childhood at the convent, and she long recognized that there was something within herself that this world could not explain. Before she had lived the last years of her life with her daughter Germaine and her family, she had lived in different apartments in many poor neighborhoods, and she had delivered babies in the shacks along the river where no human beings should live. She had grown familiar with people in all walks of life, many illiterate people with no training or family to guide them, and still they understood the concepts of honor, courage, love and duty. She was certain that there was a spirituality within a human being at birth, something that only God could conceive and plan. That is how she knew Gaudiose would come back to be with her before she died. She had not thought of him with any belief that he would return, at least, not for many years. But as she thought of him now, she realized he would come back. He would ask for her forgiveness before she died, since it was the fair and decent thing to do. And she was certain he must have missed the children and felt remorse for the life he had taken from them by his absence. But was it the fever? Was she being realistic? Had his life been happy? Perhaps when he left he never gave them another thought. But somehow, even with the fever and the inability to think clearly, she did not believe that he could suddenly stop loving the children.

Suddenly, the children were young again, and she was listening for their laughter and yearning for the way it pushed the silence of her solitary days away, if only for a moment. Time was passing and life was only a temporary segment in eternity. Fleeting images still remained of the life they had all shared together, memories of their early days of marriage when every day was like a gift. What were the sweet things Gaudiose used to say to her? She reached for the words that didn't come, and silently damned the unacceptable inevitability of senescence.

Suddenly she opened her eyes and saw her family standing and sitting in groups in the crowded room. I am still alive, she thought. How can this be? The doctors thought my death would come soon; the cancer had spread so fast. "Did Gaudiose come yet?" she asked. They rushed to her side when they realized she was awake. "Don't you see? He must come to ask my forgiveness before I die. He needs to know that I have always forgiven him. He needs to know that . . . so he can forgive himself."

Germaine spoke, "Maman, don't think of that. Are you in pain, Maman? I will get the doctor." She turned and left the room and came back in seconds with Dr. Laval.

"Are you in pain, Diana?" The doctor picked up her hand and took her pulse, then took her blood pressure reading. "I can give you something to make the pain less. It will give you a time of comfort."

"Please, Dr. Laval, I don't want anything to make me sleep. I want to be awake when he comes. Don't you see? I must be awake, because I must speak to him when my mind is clear."

"You must rest, Diana. I will give you something for the pain. It won't make you sleep." Dr. Laval, a family friend, had been caring for Germaine's mother for fourteen years, since she had come to live with them. He took them aside now and they went into the hallway where they would not be overheard.

"Your father . . . is he still alive? I believe your mother is clinging to life so she can speak with him before she dies. She won't let go, and I know at this point in her illness, her suffering is unendurable. Is there anything we can do to contact him?"

FAMILY VOICES

"Dr. Laval, we don't even know if he is still living, although if he is, his sister may know where he is. We can try." Germaine shook her auburn head with purposeful determination. She would try. She must find him, so her mother could die in peace.

A few phone calls to her father's sisters proved they were unwilling to give any information about his health or whereabouts. Germaine, Simone and Cecile were not surprised by this, but knew they must discuss what else could be done. Germaine's husband Gerry added his wisdom to the plan. The only suggestion that had merit was the one where they considered sending a false telegram to Diana informing her of Gaudiose's death. Perhaps then she could let go and die in peace. They realized then that the mother who had made a life for them in spite of the poverty and the hardships that they all endured, would soon be gone. She had refused to give up and did not allow them to stop hoping and working for a better life.

The day they sent the telegram to their mother telling her of their father's death, they knew they should say their farewells now because the telegram could arrive any minute. Germaine was the first to go in to her.

Germaine sat by her mother's bed. She picked up her mother's hand and kissed it. "Maman, I wanted you to know I have always loved you, how much we all do, and I wanted to thank you for never giving up. You enriched our lives by what you taught us. You always gave us your best, and you raised us all in a very special way. I am so sorry we didn't always have the time to show you how much we cared." She wiped her mother's forehead with a cool cloth. "We could easily have become women you would not have wanted to claim for daughters, but what did you do? You made ladies out of all of us." Germaine bent down and kissed and hugged her mother. She whispered in her mother's ear. "I should not take all of your time. Everyone is here, maman. They all want to talk to you."

Gerry always wore his emotion on his face. His eyes were wet and shiny as he came into the room. He was a handsome man, very like she remembered her husband looked, nicely trimmed mustache, full head of dark wavy hair. She touched his face as he bent his head down to kiss her.

"Thank you for my life, maman. Without the education you gave us, and all of our journeys into classical studies, our formal training in school would have been very inadequate. You opened up new worlds of meaning for all of us. You gave us a part of yourself that was rare and beautiful, and by God, we learned. You have been one glorious lady, and I love you. I have been thinking about it, and you will have to let us know what heaven is like."

"Oh, Gerry, you make me smile. I have wondered about that myself. I believe in eternity with all of my heart, my soul and my intellect. If it is possible to come back and tell you about it, I promise I will." Diana laughed to herself as she thought of it. Then the look on her face suddenly turned white and rigid, like she was preparing herself for an ongoing pain and trying not to show it.

"I'll get the doctor, maman."

"Yes, please Gerry."

Gerry left the room and Dr. Laval soon returned with a hypodermic to relieve pain.

Germaine came into the room hurriedly with a telegram in her hand. "Maman, you just received a telegram saying that Gaudiose has just died. I am so sorry. I know you hoped he would come when he heard you were ill. Perhaps he has been ill at the same time and wanted to come."

"But his sisters didn't let me know he was ill." Diana read the short telegram again and again, then her hand dropped still holding it tightly. "He is gone? I am so sorry I couldn't speak to him. I wanted him to know I forgave him for leaving. So he could forgive himself. Perhaps he knows now what I have always wanted to say. Yes, he must know, I am sure of it . . . Yes."

Diana closed her eyes and breathed a long sigh, then opened her eyes again, "Tell them all . . . all of the family, I have always loved them. They have been my life . . . And tell them good by . . . I need to rest . . . I . . . need to rest . . . I need to . . . ." Diana slipped into unconsciousness, and then she was gone.

Raymond J Beron, 24 years old

Raymond Beron and Gilberte Lachance on their wedding day, April 10 1924

Emilienne Lachance,
19 years old in a dress she designed and sewed.

Gerard Robert husband of Germain Lachance

Gerard Lachance and his wife Marie-Therese Cote

Diana Robert—age 12

Marie-Louise Pichette Robert Desjardins

Albina Boyer Desjardin—The wife of Georges Desjardin

Germaine Lachance Robert

Gaudiose Lachance-19 years old

EPILOGUE

Laurette Lachance married Adrien Girard in 1923. They lived in Montreal. They had eight children; Jean, Pierrette, Yvette, Guy, Monique, Roger, Francois, and Louise. Laurette died in January 1958 at the age of 57.

Gilberte Matilde Lachance, my mother, married Raymond J. Beron, on April 10, 1924, eight days before her nineteenth birthday. He had to wait four years for her to grow up. They lived in Proctor, a suburb of Duluth, Minnesota. They had four children, Raymond A. born on April 5, 1925, Rita J. on April 7, 1927, Richard W. born on December 11, 1929, and Giles G, on May 29, 1934. Gilberte died at the age of 52 in December, 1957.

Emiliene Lachance married Rosaire Diotte. They lived in Montreal. They had three sons, Pierre, Hubert, and Gilles. Both she and her husband lived to be in their 90s.

Gerard Lachance married MarieTherese Cote. They lived in Montreal. They had four children, Pierre, Louise, Alain, and Robert.

Germaine Lachance married Gerard Robert. They lived in Montreal most of their lives, but they lived in Trois Rivieres for a period of time also. They had a son who died shortly after birth, and two daughters, Diane and Arline.

Simone remained single and devoted herself to the family. She gave up many positions to go to family members when they needed her help because of illness or family emergencies. She took care of my mother Gilberte when she was dying of cancer in 1957.

Cecile Lachance grew healthy and strong as she grew older. She married Daniel Trudel and lived in Montreal. They had three children, Stanley, Daniel, and Caroline.

My grandmother Diana would be proud of her offspring, her grandchildren and great-grandchildren. The grandchildren have been well educated academics and successful businessmen and women. The great grandchildren have gone on to surpass all expectations in their professional careers.

Overall, the marriages of Diana's children were all lasting and successful. Not that they all were without problems, but since people have always been human, it is to be expected and is all a part of life.

I never knew either of my grandfathers. My father's father also came from Quebec, but he died in his early 50s of Tuberculosis, so I never met him.

I always had a great curiosity about my grandfather, Gaudiose Lachance. Through research of border crossings, records of employment, and some picture postcards that he had sent his children, my son in law, Dr. Norbert Hirschhorn was able to trace all of the existing records. My grandfather had changed his name and in fact, did leave Montreal with a woman named Maude. No records of remarriage were found. He was a devout Catholic, so perhaps that was never a consideration. He held several different positions in up state New York where he lived until his death in 1964. Perhaps it is the writer in me, but I was drawn to that place, and we did stop there on our way to Montreal to do research for this book. We found the old historic farm house he lived in, and we discovered a neighbor who remembered him. He was viewed as a kind man, but a man who stayed to himself. He and Maude did not mix with the other farmers in the area. He purchased milk from the neighbor we spoke to, and he often lingered there to visit. Though it was also noted that he often stayed out in his yard at the time the children walked home from school, and as they passed his house, he would call to them and talk to them. At one time he raised large Belgian Rabbits, and sometimes he would bring them out to show the children. He and Maude did not have any children, though she had a son from an earlier marriage. The neighbor we spoke to also worked with Maude. Maude was a quiet woman who never visited with others and never smiled.

Many people noticed that a man with a full head of white hair, and a white beard was openly crying in one of the pews in the back of the church at my grandmother's funeral. Several people commented on it and wondered who he was.

My grandfather Gaudiose died in 1964, ten years after my grandmother Diana's death. He had been ill for two years before he died.

ACKNOWLEDGMENTS AND RESEARCH READING

I am very grateful for the considerate assistance of the personnel at the McLennan Library at McGill University in Montreal. They were always helpful, patient and kind.

I   Canada—An Encyclopedia of the Country—Vol. I—Edited by Castel Hopkins
II   Canada and Its Provinces—Volume I—New France
III Canada and Its Provinces—Volume III British Dominion—Governing the Provinces
IV   Copp, Terry—The Anatomy of Poverty—The Condition of the Working Class in Montreal 1897 to 1929
V   Graham, Ron—The French Quarter—1992—Macfarlane, Walter and Ross—Toronto
VI   Hertzog, Stephen—A Stake in the System—Domestic Property Ownership and Social Class in Montreal 1847-1881
VII Hunter, Robert—Activite Economique—Tableau IV—Prix de detail des princepaux articles de consommation (Ville de Montreal) 1914-1915
VIII Kalm, Pehr—Pehr Kalm's Travels in North America—Volume II, English Version 1770
IX   Kestleman, Paula—The Evolution of Urban Culture Core—A Study of French Canadian Institutions and Commerce 1983

X   Lewis, Robert—Segregated City—Rent and Income—Catholic Community Services, Montreal—People of Montreal—a Bibliography of studies of their lives and behavior—1985
XI Murphy, Edward F.—Webster's Treasury of Relevant Quotations, copyright 1978 Crown Publishers
XII Olsson, Nils William—Pehr Kalm and the Image of North America
XIII Westley, Margaret—Remembrance of Grandeur: The Anglo Protestant Elite of Montreal 1900-1950 Editions Libre Expression Montreal, Quebec, Canada

FURTHER ACKNOWLEDGMENTS

The personal facts of my grandmother's life and the lives of her children were told to me in interviews with my aunts and my uncle over the years, and their children and what they remember of things that their mothers shared with them of the intimate details of their lives. The last fourteen years of my grandmother's life she lived with her daughter Germaine and her husband their two children, Diane and Arline. Diane gave me the details of our grandmother's early life with the Desjardins for she spent many afternoons over a cup of tea, talking to our grandmother about her early life during the time she lived with them.

My mother Gilberte discussed her life after her father left, but only when I was in high school. I had believed when I was young that her father had died. She did not confide the truth until I was older. Then she could not speak of the details without crying. I listened to these stories with sadness for I finally understood what the family had suffered during those years.

I have one regret. I had a difficult time finding photos of all of the family, particularly when the children were young. I was told that there was a lovely old family album (velvet cover) that Emilienne took to the nursing home where she was cared for during the last few years of her life. It was never found after she died. Photos of all of the children and family pictures would have enriched the story.

Rita Beron Myntti

SYNOPSIS OF FAMILY VOICES

Diana Roberts is sent to live with a wealthy great uncle when she is four years old in 1885. She is educated like a princess, and when her aunt dies just before her graduation in 1899, she is forced into an arranged marriage because of the social mores of the times.

In 1915, her husband leaves her when she is pregnant for the seventh child. There are no governmental assistance programs in l915 for widowed or abandoned families, and it is a story of the struggle and how the family copes. Child labor is rampant, and the oldest girls who are 12 and 14 are forced to work 12 hour days, six days a week, for little money. Diana teaches them at home, becomes a midwife, teaches piano lessons and anything she can do to keep them together. How the children try to protect their mother from the realities of their lives and Diana's struggle to make a life for them is the main theme of the book. The story is based on the true facts of their lives.

Rita J. Beron

NORMANDALE COMMUNITY COLLEGE
LIBRARY
9700 FRANCE AVENUE SOUTH
BLOOMINGTON, MN 55431-4399